THE BEAR AND THE ROSE

THE BEAR AND THE ROSE

Connor MacKenzie

LBME Publishing

The Bear and The Rose
LBME Publishing: http://LBMEPublishing.com/
ISBN: 978-1-64676-008-4 (trade paperback)
ISBN: 978-1-64676-009-1 (ebook)

First Edition

Printed in the United States of America.

This story is dedicated to:
the Real-Life Rosie—she knows who she is.

ACKNOWLEDGMENTS

My Twitch Tank Crew

J. T. "Jack" Shennaghy

FemaleWriter

Bob Watkins

EmperorOfFinland for his insights
on the Soviet Satellites of the 1960s

Kessahara, aka Duckie

Mayah Robinson

Special thanks to Sofilein: Livestreamer, Youtuber, and Tank Dork Extraordinaire, for her outstanding tour of the M2 Bradley Fighting Vehicle with JB. Please follow her on YouTube.

Many thanks to the LPA—Little People of America, especially their publication It's a Whole New View—A Guide for Raising a Child with Dwarfism by Joanna Campbell & Nina Dorren.

And, as always, my heartfelt thanks to Lon Böder and Penney Knightly for the many hours of brainstorming and all the encouragement and support, without which this volume would never have come to be.

TABLE OF CONTENTS

– Chapter 1 –

Day Twelve

"**S**TOP! IN THE name of the Loward, we order you to stop and surrender!"

Forget that, Rosie thought, and sprinted as fast as she could manage along the rain-drenched street.

"Stop, I said! We are the Loward's Fury! We order you to stop at once and submit to our authority!"

Fat chance. Rosie ran even faster, her rubber-soled sneakers raising a misty wake behind her. *So much for my glorious adventure. I didn't expect it to end this way—not so soon, at least.*

* * *

It had been easier to leave her home, such as it was, than she had expected. For two weeks, she had saved up her daily dose of 'medicine,' the drugs they gave her to 'help her stay calm.' Then she spiked her parents' nighttime herbal tea with them. As soon as they had passed out on the couch, she packed a small daypack with what little food there was in the house, a spare top, a spare pair of jeans, a change of underwear, her all-organic toothbrush, and an old olive-green woolen army blanket that would serve as her bedroll. Her dad told her it probably had been used by a soldier during the War.

She put on her best jeans, which were only a tiny bit ragged, a sweatshirt, and a light jacket, the only jacket she had. She shivered, removed the jacket, put on her raveled cable-knit sweater, then replaced the jacket. Better.

She patted her front pants pocket, double-checking that her folding knife was there. Her grandfather had gifted it to her before he passed away six years ago when Rosie was only eight.

After a moment's reflection, she slipped her bra out from under her shirt and draped it over her father's face. He'd been such a jerk that one time she went bra-less at home. He'd ranted on and on about 'modest' dress for young women and 'conducting one's self properly in the eyes of the Loward', and how such misconduct wasn't 'uplifting.' She couldn't imagine how he'd even noticed—she'd been wearing this same sweater. Well, if he liked her bra so much, he could keep it. It never fit right, anyway.

As usual, her mother had said nothing in Rosie's defense, just sat there, gazing off into la-la land, tears streaming down her face. Mother didn't handle conflict very well. She was willing to sacrifice anything and everything to avoid angering Father, including Rosie, her only child. She called it 'being in subjection to the Loward,' but, to Rosie, it looked suspiciously like a lack of backbone.

She left her neighborhood, Diablo, for the last time, just a few minutes past midnight. Diablo was a tiny smattering of houses that had, for reasons that would forever remain unclear, avoided destruction during the catastrophic War of Righteousness. Or so she had been told, anyway—the War had happened many years before she was born. She wouldn't miss Diablo, that was for sure: it was a dirty, impoverished circle of half-ruined hovels inhabited largely by ignorant hillbillies, including her parents and the other members of their idiot 'Church of the Loward.'

Her first priority had been to find a structure not fully collapsed to use as a hiding place the following day. That wasn't anywhere nearly as easy as it sounded—most of the area had been completely flattened during the War. Very few buildings remained standing between Diablo and the Old Downtown area of Ritual City.

Rosie had planned to travel only at night, after it was fully dark, to avoid the Scavs and the bands of Johnson's Militia that hunted them. Also, the Angels of the Loward, the enforcement arm of her parents' church. They weren't called that anymore, though; now they called themselves The Loward's Fury and had become aggressive and vicious. She wasn't sure which was worse, the Militia, the Loward's Fury, or the Scavs, and she wasn't interested in finding out. Her sole purpose was to reach Old City, the former downtown, where Johnson himself was organizing his followers, or so she had heard from the kids at church and school. She was sure that Johnson would welcome her into the fold, and all would be well from then on. All she had to do was get there.

It had proven much more problematic than she had anticipated. She had eaten her entire food supply on that first night, huddling in a dark corner that was the only remaining portion of a flattened house just a half-mile from her home. Since then, she had salvaged a few odd cans of food from among the ruined houses. The Scavs had carted off nearly everything worth salvaging long ago, but a careful search sometimes revealed a stray can or two.

Rosie was used to eating very little because the bizarre, nameless Loward her parents worshipped required strict veganism. Extreme poverty didn't help much, either, in terms of keeping the pantry stocked. Even so, if she didn't find something to eat pretty soon, she'd be too weak to walk, and that would be the end of it. Last night, the eleventh night since leaving home, she had been too tired and hungry to scavenge, so she simply crawled into one of the ruined houses, wrapped her blanket around her, and went immediately to sleep.

She slept long past sunrise until the feeble warmth of the autumn sun heated the ruined house a bit. This was her twelfth day since leaving Diablo. She was too weak to walk, nearly too weak to get to her feet. Shivering, she forced her shaking legs to stand, wrapped her scanty blanket around herself as best she could, then sifted through the debris that covered the floor of the old house, just as it covered the floors of all the other houses she'd seen so far. There was a word, a special word, for the debris... 'kibble?' No, that was cat food. Her parents used to feed vegan kibble to the cat—probably what killed it in the end. It was vegan—vegetarian—kibble, and cats needed meat, right? Rosie didn't know where her parents had gotten the vegetarian kibble. It came in a brown paper sack with grease stains all over it, and the words 'cat food' scrawled in shaky handwriting on it. It smelled kind of funky, but if Rosie closed her eyes, it tasted a little like summer squash. Maybe it was made from squash, for all Rosie knew. Better than starving, anyway, though she felt a little guilty for stealing the cat's food.

'Kipple'—yes, that was the word she was thinking of. She'd read it once in a tattered pre-War paperback book she had found in a house back in Diablo, written by some ancient writer about a time that seemed to Rosie to be very much like now.* She had sneaked the book into her room and hidden it under a loose floorboard, reading it only on the rare occasions that both of her parents were out of the house. Her father was illiterate; her mother knew how to read, but didn't—she didn't consider reading 'worldly literature' to be 'uplifting.' In the story—Rosie didn't remember the name of it—the world was drowning in kipple, the leftover bits of an abandoned world where no one was left to pick up stuff and throw it away. Empty matchbook covers were one component of the kipple in the story. Rosie remembered the mention of matchbook covers, even though she had no idea what they were. Anyway, the floor of this house was covered in kipple. Rosie liked the sound of the word, and she said it out loud several times, "kipple... kipple... kipple..." just to feel it roll off her tongue.

As she had moved westward toward the old downtown sector of Ritual City, the houses had become progressively older. She figured this one was over a hundred years old, probably built long before the War of Righteousness. Or maybe they were built after some other previous war, she thought, for the soldiers who were coming home to raise families in. She wondered how many

---

* Do Androids Dream of Electric Sheep, Philip K. Dick, 1968

times in the history of the world soldiers had come home from one war or another and needed places to live.

Rosie gave up on searching the floor. In addition to the kipple, the floor was covered in dirt, dust, and rat droppings, and smelled like rat pee. Instead, she went to poke through the kitchen cabinets, not really expecting to find anything. She was amazed to find an old can of beans that had tipped over and rolled to the back corner of a lopsided cabinet shelf. Probably why the Scavs missed it. She never would have spotted it in the dark.

The expiration date on the can was so far back that she laughed out loud. Well, can't have everything, right? It was the first time she ever used the can-opener blade on her pocket knife. It was harder than she had expected. She made a small, ragged opening in the can's lid, then sniffed the contents carefully. The beans smelled okay. She made the opening larger and tasted them, cautiously, at first. They tasted good, very good. She went back to her daypack and retrieved a spoon, then devoured the entire can. A few moments later, when she suffered no apparent ill effects, she wandered out into what had once been someone's backyard, but now was overgrown with shrubs and bushes, and took care of her necessary body functions. She was happy that she'd had the foresight to pack a couple of rolls of sanitary paper.

She took a deep breath of the chill autumn air. Overall, she was feeling much better. Energized, even! Ready for a Bright New Day! Or night, rather. Amazing, the restorative power of one little can of outdated beans! She packed her bedroll and the utensils. It was time to get a move on, time to hit the road. It was almost sundown and an approaching storm front enhanced the safety of night. The crescent-shaped bands of clouds had been getting thicker and darker all afternoon. Rosie hoped she'd find the next day's shelter before the rain started.

It didn't work out that way, though. Soon after she left the ruined house, it began to drizzle, then to rain in earnest. By sundown she was soaked to the skin, freezing cold, and miserable. The small boost she'd gotten from the beans had long since passed. She trudged along, head down, into the driving wind and rain until well past midnight without finding a resting place. She walked through a completely flattened neighborhood and came out at the edge of what had once been a minor thoroughfare.

And that's when the Loward's Fury had spotted her.

* * *

"Last chance! Freeze and surrender or we'll cut you down!"

Rosie dashed across the nameless thoroughfare and dived into a shallow ditch that ran along a ruined iron fence.

Without hesitation, she thrashed her way along the ditch, overgrown with weeds and surging with rain runoff. She forced her exhausted body against the current as fast as she could. But she knew she wouldn't be able to keep it up for long. When she could run no more, she stuck her head up to see if the Fury were still following.

"There she is! Shoot her!"

She ducked back down into the ditch as bullets whizzed over her head. The boots of the Fury pounded on the wet asphalt only a few yards behind her. Then the worst came to pass: the little ditch ran out. She launched herself onto the roadway and across the thoroughfare, where she ran headlong into an enormous bushy hedge, over twice her height. It was nearly invisible in the rain and dark and seemed to go on down the thoroughfare as far as she could see, which wasn't very far.

Defeated, she stopped and raised her hands above her head. *So this is how it ends*, she thought. *Still better than slowly starving to death in Diablo.*

The Loward's Fury patrol comprised six young men in black uniforms decorated with silver angels. They surrounded Rosie in a semi-circle, aiming their assault rifles at her. She backed up against the hedge.

"Well, well, what have we here?" the apparent squad leader asked in the voice common to horse's backsides the world over. "If it isn't a little girl! What are you doing out here, all alone in the middle of the night, Baby Sister?"

Rosie tried to peer through the hedge, but she saw nothing except blackness. "Noth… nothing…" she said, teeth chattering.

She edged sideways along the gnarled and twisted hedge for a few feet until one of the Fury motioned with his rifle for her to stop. She stopped, having seen no way through the hedge.

The squad leader approached. "What's in the backpack, Baby Sister? Running away from home, perhaps? You know the Loward wouldn't approve." He reached for the backpack, but Rosie grabbed the straps and held on tight, to no avail. The squad leader ripped the little pack off her shoulders and began rifling through the contents.

"You must be the missing girl from Diablo. You know that we're going to have to take you home, Baby Sister, don't you? The Loward doesn't approve of runaways. Of course, you'll have to come back to headquarters with us guys, first, for a little 'socialization.'"

"That's never going to happen! I'll die first!" Out of the corner of her eye, Rosie spied a pair of bright eyes looking up at her from the bottom of the hedge, accompanied by a pair of very long pink ears. Without hesitation, she snatched her pack out of the squad leader's hands and plunged headlong into the hedge, which seemed to be made entirely of long, sharp thorns.

Shots rang out! Bullets clipped the leaves of the hedge, then she felt a blow on her right side. She wriggled harder, ignoring painful jabs from the thorns. Turning this way and that, she forced her way through the hedge and fell face-first into a patch of tall grass.

She chuckled to herself: it wasn't likely that the Fury soldiers would follow her through that tangled hedge. She ignored the pain in her side, forced herself to her feet, and ran like the wind into the darkness. The firing continued behind her, but the bullets weren't coming anywhere close, now.

Rosie ran blindly through the grass. She couldn't see anything at all, just blackness. The firing behind her continued, so Rosie just kept on running, until *Bam!* She ran right into a solid wall.

A solid wall made of fur. Fur? She felt to her left, then to her right, and there was nothing but fur. Had she run into a wild animal? A bear? A really *big* bear! Her knees sagged, but the bear grabbed her shoulders and pulled her upright.

And that's when, way off in the distance, she heard the dogs bark. Rosie wasn't afraid of dogs, exactly, but she wasn't all that comfortable with them, either. She hadn't known many dogs in her fourteen years, and most of the ones she had met had been of the "fits in the palm of your hand" variety. Disgusting little yap-rats. She ventured a guess that the two dogs producing the long, deep howls and growls she was hearing were definitely *not* yap-rats. *Much* larger, Rosie guessed. She shivered again.

With a crack like thunder, several extremely bright lights came on high above her. Were they up in trees? Or maybe on poles? They washed Rosie, the grass, and the now-distant hedge with a cold, actinic, white light. The instant the lights came on, the firing from the hedge ceased.

Rosie shook herself loose from the bear and backed up a few steps. She squinted against the brightness and covered her eyes with her hands, blinking and occasionally peeking through her fingers.

Ack! Approaching her across the lawn were two smaller bears. They, too, were covered in long, dark, wet fur. Rosie was petrified. She told her feet to Run! Run for our life! But her feet just stood there in the grass, doing nothing at all. Her knees were knocking, and she thought she was going to pee herself. *Well, so what if I do?* she thought, somewhat irrelevantly. *No one would even notice in this weather.*

The two bears stopped next to the big bear. They looked at Rosie for a while, lips drawn back, growling. Then the big bear said something to the two little bears, who sat down in the wet grass. The big bear very slowly approached Rosie, making calming gestures with its paws.

The calming gestures weren't working, Rosie observed in an oddly detached manner, then went right ahead and peed herself. She had been correct—the bear didn't even seem to notice.

The big bear kept inching closer… closer… its black beady eyes peering out at her through its thick, black, fur. When it was directly in front of her again, the bear stopped. Slowly, slowly, it raised its paws and—pushed back its hood? The bear was wearing a hood! Oddly, it didn't look much different with the hood pulled back. It lowered its paws, opened its mouth, and… spoke! "Well, come on, then. We'd better get you out of this rain."

Then the bear turned and walked away from Rosie. The two smaller bears followed the big bear. Rosie, still rooted to the spot, watched them disappear into the blackness behind the giant lights. A long moment later, the big bear appeared again. "Well? You comin' or what?" Then it turned and disappeared once more.

Rosie shouted, "Wait! Wait for me! I'm coming!" But at last, the loss of blood took over, and she sank to the ground.

The bear was instantly by her side. "What is it? What's the matter?"

Rosie said quietly, "I think… I may have been shot." And then she passed out.

— Chapter 2 —

Mr. The Bear

Rosie clenched her eyes tight against the glare of the over-head light. She lay on her back, her shirt pulled up above her belly. She blinked a few times, then tried to swing her legs off the table.

"Better to stay put, for the moment, anyway." A gentle, soothing, deep voice.

"Where… where am I? Who are you? What am I doing here?"

"Easy does it," the gentle voice advised. "One question at a time, if you please. In the order in which you asked: one: you are lying on a medical examination table in the nurse's office of my home. Two: I'm a doctor. Three: you are getting a hole in your side stitched up. Best you lie still while I'm stitching."

"I'm cold," Rosie said, shivering. She realized she was wrapped in a blanket above where he was working. Another blanket covered her below. She pulled the top blanket a little tighter around her.

"I don't doubt it. You were soaked to the skin when I found you. Plus, you've been shot, it seems. You're probably in shock and hypothermic. We can fix those, but not while you're bleeding out. Gotta get that wound closed first."

Bear gave Rosie a small hand mirror. "You can watch what I'm doing if you like. Makes some people queasy, though."

Rosie aimed the mirror so she could see where the stitches were going in. She surreptitiously slid a hand under the bottom blanket. "Hey! Where's my pants?" She checked under the top blanket. "Where are the rest of my clothes?"

"I took them off. They were soaking wet. Can't get you warm if you're soaking wet, right?"

He noticed the blush creeping into Rosie's cheeks. "It's okay, I'm a doctor. Or, at least, I was a doctor before the War. I've seen plenty of naked people, male, female, young, old, you name it. It's part of the job. We'll get you some dry clothes as soon as I'm done here."

Rosie thought this over. "I guess it doesn't matter much. Back home, I wasn't allowed to be body-shy. I always took showers and even used the toilet with the bathroom door open. Mother, too. Daddy said God required it, that privacy was an invitation to sin."

"Hmm," was all that Bear said. He finished with the sutures, applied some antiseptic lotion, and covered the wound with a waterproof bandage. "All done. No, don't get up. Just lie there quietly for a bit. I'm going to find you some antibiotic. I'll be back in a few minutes. Molly and Bruno will stay with you."

"Molly and Bruno?"

"The dogs. You met them outside. Don't you remember?"

Rosie thought hard. "I remember bears. One big one and two little ones. I guess maybe you were the big one."

He smiled kindly. "Yep, that's me. I guess I am sort of a bear. My friends actually call me 'Bear.' You can call me Bear, too, if you want to. As for the dogs—they *are* dogs—they might as well be bears. They're a breed called Newfoundlands, wonderful dogs."

Rosie looked at the two huge black shaggy dogs who were sniffing her politely. "I guess you two were the little bears, weren't you?"

Molly and Bruno wagged their tails furiously. Rosie reached out and patted Molly on the head. "Nice to meet you, Molly. You too, Bruno. I'm Rosie."

Bear smiled, and, for the first time in twelve days, so did Rosie. More than twelve days, really, though. A lot more.

Bear said, "You're in good hands. Or paws, rather. I'm going to get some penicillin. Five minutes, tops." He turned and went out the door.

The dogs settled down on the rug to wait for the return of their master. Rosie took the opportunity to look around the room. Two beds occupied the center of the main room. She was on a treatment table of some sort near a group of cabinets. A few straight-backed chairs and a couple of long couches completed the furnishings. A door led to a small bathroom. She made out part of a sink and a toilet in the half-light.

How peculiar to find a place like this in the middle of the ruins! It was a good thing she did, though, or those Loward's Furies would have killed her. Or worse. She shivered again. *Close call,* she thought.

She must have dozed off for a moment, because when she opened her eyes again, Bear was standing over her. "Uh-uh, no sleeping. Sleep is not good for people in shock. Sorry I took so long—I decided to make a detour over to the gym to find some dry clothes. First, though, we'd better get this penicillin into you."

And, so saying, he produced a syringe, filled it from a small bottle in his pocket, and held it up to the light to check the dosage. Then he tapped the cylinder and squirted a bit of the white fluid into the air. "Ready?"

"Will it hurt?"

"Hurt? Oh, yes, it'll hurt like the blazes!"

"Really?"

"No, not really."

Rosie held out her arm and squinched her eyes shut. "Okay, I'm ready."

"You're already done," Bear said. "I put it in your hip when you weren't looking."

"I didn't feel anything at all!"

Bear laughed. "Haven't lost my touch yet, I guess! Now, let's see if I can treat your hypothermia. Wrap that blanket around your shoulders. Can you stand up? Yes, good, that's right. Now, little steps into the bathroom. Good."

Bear started the shower running. Rosie started to take off the blanket, but Bear motioned for her to wait. "It takes a moment to run hot." He put an old football jersey on the counter by the sink. "Now here's what I want you to do: take yourself a shower, for as long and hot as you can stand it. It's not good if you get cold too deep inside, because you can't warm yourself up again. It's called hypothermia, and it's dangerous, can even kill you. Understand?"

Rosie nodded.

"When you're done," Bear continued, "you can put on that football jersey. It's number 47, an excellent number. It's long enough to cover you top and bottom. You call me if you need me, or if you feel dizzy, okay?"

"Okay. Aren't you going to stay with me?"

"Nope. I'm not body-shy, either, but in Bear Country it's customary for young ladies to bathe themselves in private."

"But you already saw me—"

"That was for medical purposes. Not the same thing. Now get yourself warmed up. Take as long as you want. Towels are in this cabinet." He left, closing the bathroom door behind him.

Rosie was in heaven. She hadn't had more than a few handfuls of water to bathe in at any one time since she was a tiny girl. She barely remembered having showers and even tub baths with her mother. Then the droughts came, water was rationed, then restricted, then it dried up altogether. After that, the Diablo residents dug a well of their own, but it was dry a lot of the time. Rosie and her mother and father had mostly washed out of a bucket when there was enough water to wash at all. She edged the hot water valve up another notch, then rinsed her hair. It felt so *good*!

When she was thoroughly warmed, inside and out, Rosie turned the shower off and squeezed the excess water out of her shoulder-length blond hair. She wrapped one towel around her hair in that special way only girls can do. She dried herself thoroughly with a second towel, then pulled the old football jersey over her head. It came down to her knees. She wiped the steam off the mirror and inspected her face. Well, it was what it was. She wondered where her comb might be, or if Mr. The Bear had one. She opened the bathroom door to find Bear sitting quietly on one of the upright wooden chairs.

"Feeling better?" Bear asked. "Nice and warm, all the way inside?" He stared at the towel piled on her head. It had been a long time, a *very* long time, since Bear had seen a female do that trick with a towel. He wondered how girls learned those things. Was it instinctive, or was there some secret Girl Society that passed on arcane feminine knowledge and secrets? Or maybe there was a rule book for females?

"Um…" Rosie hesitated.

"What is it?" Bear asked.

"I need a comb," Rosie said. "I had a backpack…"

"You still do," Bear said. He retrieved Rosie's backpack and wet clothes from a corner of the room. "I brought it in while you were unconscious. Is it okay if I look inside?"

Rosie marveled at his courtesy—no one had ever asked her permission before. "Um… sure. I don't mind. Can I help?"

"Of course, you can help," Bear said. "It's your stuff. How about we spread it out on the table here?"

Rosie nodded, and Bear carefully emptied the contents of the backpack onto the table, then offered a chair to Rosie and pulled one up for himself.

"Everything's soaking wet," Rosie said, dismayed. "I think my toilet paper is a goner."

"It's okay," Bear said. "We have plenty here, all nice and dry." He chuckled to himself. "My dad had a thing about toilet paper before the War of Righteousness. He used to say, 'There are a lot of things I'd rather be without than toilet paper.'"

Rosie laughed. "Sounds right to me. Did your father die in the War?"

"No, he died quite some time before the war. He was a soldier in the war before the War of Righteousness, and in the war before that. When I was born, he was well into his forties, and quite old when I grew up—like being raised by a grandfather. He didn't live long enough to see the War of Righteousness. Which was just as well."

Rosie considered this. "I didn't know about the wars before the War. Have there always been wars?"

"Always," Bear said sadly. "No one ever wants them, but they happen anyway. Makes no sense, really."

Rosie sorted the wet things from her pack and piled them together with the wet clothes she had been wearing. The other items, including her comb, she left on the table.

Bear suggested, "There's a washing machine and dryer in the utility room." He pointed through a doorway on the other side of the room. "They used it for washing sheets and towels and such. If you'd like, we can wash and dry your clothes."

"Yes, please," Rosie said. "I've never seen a washing machine. At Diablo, Mother washed our stuff in a tub out in the yard when there was enough water. I helped her when I got bigger."

"This is a lot easier," Bear said, as he scooped up the wet clothes and carried them off to the washer. Rosie watched, fascinated, as Bear dumped in the clothes, added some detergent, closed the lid, and twiddled the dials. When the machine started running, they went back to sit at the table.

Rosie arranged her few remaining belongings: comb, knife, saturated toilet paper, two rolls, and a few other odds and ends. Shyly, she handed Bear the big comb, then folded her hands in her lap and waited.

Bear stared at her. After a moment, she looked up at Bear inquiringly. Bear unstuck himself from his momentary paralysis and began combing Rosie's hair, gently working out the tangles according to a long-forgotten method he once knew. He brushed incipient tears from his eyes with the back of his hand. *Dang!* he thought, *no good can come of this.* There were things he just didn't want to remember. *Steady on,* he told himself, *there's no way she could know.*

When the combing had been accomplished, Bear and Rosie gathered her things. Bear guided Rosie to a mirror where he received the Rosie Seal of Approval for his combing technique. "We'll come back in an hour and switch your clothes to the dryer. Meanwhile, I expect you could do with a bite to eat."

Rosie nodded enthusiastically, so Bear led her out of the nurse's office into the outside corridor, turned right, then right again, and headed down a long concrete pathway.

26

— Chapter 3 —

Holly Oakes High

As they walked, Rosie peered around, but couldn't see much in the dark. "What place is this, Mr. The Bear?"

"It's an old high school, abandoned long before the War. It went up for tax auction, and I bought it."

"What's a high school?"

"Don't you go to school?"

"We have something we call a school back in my old neighborhood, but it isn't very high. It's just a house. Or what's left of a house. There are six or seven of us kids. We sit in a circle, and one of the grown-ups tells us stuff."

"I see. Well, this school was for students around the ages of 14 to 18, who had already learned the basics of reading and writing. But there hadn't been many kids that age in this neighborhood for a long time before the War, so they closed it down."

"I'm fourteen," said Rosie, "and I can read and write. And do maths, too. I like to read, but I wasn't allowed to read anything much except the Old Bible and the Word of the Loward." She sighed.

"I bet you didn't let that stop you," Bear said, grinning.

Rosie grinned back. "Not so much," she said, and blushed. "What was it called?"

"The school?"

Rosie nodded.

"Holly Oaks High School. It was named, incorrectly, after the oak trees we have here in the Big Valley."

"Why incorrectly?"

"Because Holly Oaks only grow in Europe, around the Mediterranean Sea. You know: Spain, Italy, France, and so forth. But the early settlers in Ritual City thought the valley oaks were Holly Oaks, which, in all fairness, they do look somewhat alike. Ironic, that a place of learning should be named incorrectly, don't you think?"

"I don't know any of those places," Rosie said. "This is the first time I've ever been away from Diablo."

"Is that where you lived? Diablo? You walked all the way from Diablo? That's over eight miles from here!"

"It took me twelve days, though. I had to go slowly through the ruins. And I only walked at night."

"Because of Scavs?"

"And Johnson's Militia, too, but mostly the Loward's Fury. I was very careful not to be seen."

"I've heard about the Loward's Fury," Bear said. "Didn't they call themselves the Angels of the Loward?"

Rosie nodded. "Until a little while ago, a few months, maybe. Then the Most High Quaestor—he calls himself the Iron Sceptre—took over and changed the name to the Loward's Fury. Before that, they went around making sure everyone was dressed modestly and eating vegan. But after they became the Fury, they got uniforms and guns and started being mean to people. Also, hunting down runaways, like me, and taking them home again. Which might sound fine to you, but the ones who cornered me last night said they were going to take me to their headquarters and have some fun with me first."

Bear said nothing, but his face turned dark and he scowled in a way that made Rosie shiver.

"Don't worry, Mr. The Bear," Rosie soothed. "I would have died before I went with them."

Bear's scowl deepened. "It's not nice to treat little girls that way," he growled. "It's not nice to treat *anyone* that way."

They walked together in silence for a few dozen yards, then arrived at a pair of double glass doors. "This used to be the school cafeteria," Bear said.

"What's a cafeteria?"

"It's a place for a lot of people to eat together. Back when Holly Oaks was still in operation, students could buy lunch here, or bring a lunch from home and eat it here with their fellow students. Sometimes there were performances, too." Bear pointed at a small, raised platform that had once served as a makeshift stage for the drama department's presentations.

Rosie marveled at the sheer number of tables and chairs in the room. She'd never in her life seen that many people together at one time. "How many students were there?"

"Oh, around 2,400. There were four grades, with about 600 in each grade."

Rosie strained to picture what the cafeteria had been like when it was filled with students. Did they talk and laugh? Or did they eat in silence, like she did at home? She couldn't imagine what that many students would sound like if they all talked at the same time.

Bear escorted Rosie to the actual kitchen portion of the building, where she, wide-eyed, took stock of the gleaming stainless-steel sinks, cabinets, tables, ranges, and other commercial kitchen equipment.

"Well," Bear said, "what'll you have?" He pointed at a large faded menu sign above the serving line, with pictures of various dishes.

Rosie was dumbfounded. She had no clue what was available or what she might request. She didn't recognize any of the pictures on the menu. Finally, she pointed at one of the pictures at random.

Bear frowned, puzzled. "Cheeseburgers? Seriously? I thought you said you were vegan?"

"I said my *parents* were vegan."

"What are you, then?"

"Pretty doggoned hungry!"

Bear laughed. "We can fix that!" He threw four burger patties on the grill. Bruno and Molly, attracted by the smell of the burgers cooking, trotted up to Bear with expectant faces. Bear laughed again and threw another couple of burgers on the grill. Both tails wagged furiously.

Rosie laughed. "I guess they've had burgers before?"

"From time to time, on special occasions."

"Special occasions? Like what?"

"Like whenever we feel like it."

Rosie laughed again. She had a cute laugh, Bear noted.

Bear plated up the burgers, two for Rosie, one each for Bruno and Molly, and two for himself. He set Rosie's plate on the table, then fetched ketchup and mustard. Then went back for relish, onion and tomato slices, and some lettuce.

Rosie hesitated.

"Want me to show you?" Bear asked.

Rosie nodded.

Bear opened the burgers, added onion on top of the cheese, then ketchup. Next, the tomato, the relish, and the lettuce. The mustard went on the top half of the bun, which topped the stack.

Rosie stared. She couldn't recall ever seeing that much food at a single meal. Not ever.

"What's the matter?" Bear asked. "I thought you were hungry."

"I… I… I… am—" And she started to cry.

Bear gave her a moment, then went over and sat beside her. "Here, let me help you. Do like I do." He picked up one of the burgers using both of his bear-paw-sized hands, then kind of smooshed it down.

Rosie did the same with her burger.

"Now open your mouth as wide as it will go. Wider… wider… that's it. Okay, now shove the burger in as far as it will go, then take the biggest bite you can."

Rosie did as instructed. A significant portion of cheeseburger vanished into her gaping maw.

"Outstanding!" Bear roared. "That is the girl!"

Rosie was motionless for a few seconds, then slowly started chewing. Chewing and smiling, smiling wider and chewing harder. At last, the first bite of burger left the scene and headed for her stomach. Rosie started crying again.

"What's the matter? No good? You don't like it? I can make you something else."

"No… I like it. I just… never had anything so good before in my life. I didn't even *know* food could taste good. My mother said food wasn't supposed to taste good, it was just supposed to be fuel."

"Poor, sad, unfortunate woman," Bear said. "Sucks to be her, I guess."

Rosie smiled. "I guess!" She took another huge bite, closed her eyes, and chewed blissfully.

When the burgers were gone, Rosie swiped the ketchup off the plate with a finger, then licked her finger clean. She sighed a long, happy, contented sigh.

"Shall I make you another one?" Bear asked.

"Oh, no, Mr. The Bear, I couldn't possibly. I'm not used to eating that much and I'm stuffed! Look at my tummy!" She pulled her jersey up far enough to display her bulging belly. "If I put something more in there, I think I'd explode."

They laughed together. Bear pointed out an ancient, faded poster that hung on the wall, entitled *The Five Basic Food Groups*. "There you are! According to that chart, the cheeseburger is the perfect food: the patty is meat, the cheese is dairy, the bun is carbohydrate, the lettuce is vegetables, and the tomato is fruit, technically. See? Yay, cheeseburger!"

Rosie studied the poster. "I see… yes. Perfect! I wonder why my parents don't know about this? If they saw me eat a cheeseburger, they'd fall down dead."

"Ever heard of Pizza?"

Rosie shook her head.

"Another perfect food. Tomorrow, if you like, I'll show you pizza."

"I'd like that," Rosie said. "But I'm afraid…" She yawned a huge yawn.

Bear peered into her wide-open mouth. "I think I can see that second cheeseburger."

Rosie laughed, then blinked sleepily.

"Come on, let's find you a place to sleep."

Bear took her back to the nurse's office, with Molly and Bruno bouncing along behind them. It was clear that the dogs liked Bear's new friend. Before they entered, Rosie pointed to several other doors in the same building. "Where do those go?"

"To what used to be the principal's and vice-principal's offices. They were the leaders, the bosses, of the high school. This entire wing, including the nurse's office, was called the Administration Building."

"And what about that building across the courtyard?"

"It was the school library. It's full of books. I'll show later if you like."

"Yes, please."

Inside, Bear pointed at one of the two patients' beds near the middle of the room. "You can sleep there."

Rosie fell into it and was instantly asleep. Bear covered her with a blanket. The dogs curled up on the floor next to Rosie's bed.

— Chapter 4 —

WHAT'S ON YOUR MIND?

WHEN BEAR WOKE up late in the morning, Rosie was still asleep. He got up quietly and wrote Rosie a note saying that he'd be back in a little while and left it on the table by her bed. Then he took the dogs out for their morning walk through the compound.

As the dogs frolicked in the dewy grass, Bear considered his situation. After decades of a relatively peaceful life as a hermit, he was suddenly—no, *abruptly*—in charge of a fourteen-year-old runaway.

Where is she going? What does she want? She doesn't seem too smart—no, that's not right—she seems smart enough, but not very well informed. Well, okay, we're all like that when we're born, most of us, anyway: we have a working brain but we're lacking information and experience.

That was it: Rosie was lacking information and experience. Bear could do something about that, he supposed. But should he? Was it even any of his business? He sighed and threw a couple of well-worn tennis balls for the dogs.

Should he keep Rosie as a pet? Or perhaps as a student? Or merely patch her up and send her on her way? A lot would depend on Rosie herself, what she wanted. He wasn't about to become her jailer, no matter what.

Well, there was only one way to find out what was on the kid's mind. First, though, he should get some breakfast into her. Everything is better after coffee, right? Of course, it is. He called Bruno and Molly and went down to the cafeteria to whip up a couple of omelets, some apples, and a large flask of coffee, all of which he carried back to the nurse's office.

Rosie was awake. She'd washed her face, and made some attempt at combing out her hair. She still had bed face and looked slightly tousled, but she seemed okay. At least she smiled when Bear cautiously entered the room.

"Good morning, Mr. The Bear," Rosie said.

"Good morning to you, Rosie the Girl. Are you hungry?"

"Starving!"

"I brought some breakfast. Come sit at the table with me. Did you sleep well?"

"I did. This is the softest bed I've ever slept on. Plus, I was pretty tired."

"That'll do it." Bear frowned. "But the beds in here aren't that soft—they made them hard and uncomfortable on purpose back then, before the War, you know. The idea was to encourage sick kids not to linger about."

Rosie laughed. "That's weird. Kinda backwards, maybe." She shrugged. "I don't know much about before the War."

Bear nodded slowly. "Probably the most significant thing to know about the pre-War times is the sheer number of people there were back then. This school was full of students, hundreds of them. The neighborhoods you walked through? They were filled with people. Every house had a family living in it. There were always cars on the streets, lots of them. It seemed like everybody was always going somewhere."

"Even at night?"

"Even at night. I've seen the freeway out by Diablo jammed up bumper-to-bumper at four o'clock in the morning."

Rosie was stumped. "What's a freeway? What's a bumper-to-bumper?"

Now Bear was stumped. "A freeway is a really big street for lots of cars. Bumper-to-bumper is a way of not getting anywhere fast."

"I don't get it."

"Nor I," Bear admitted.

Rosie sniffed at the coffee flask. "What's this?"

"Coffee. Haven't you had coffee before?"

"My parents didn't believe—"

"—in drinking coffee. Loward's Own stuff again, right?"

"Yeah."

"Did they ever say why?"

"No, just that God wouldn't like it."

"What do you think?"

"I think I want to try some. What is it, exactly?"

"It's a beverage—a drink—made from the seeds of the coffee tree. The seeds are roasted, ground, and brewed or steeped in water."

"Steeped? Like tea?"

"Similar. Coffee contains caffeine, a mild stimulant. For people my age, coffee is an important boost in the morning."

"What about people *my* age?"

"People your age like it, too. It's not like getting high, it just energizes you a little. It's easy to make. If you want, I'll show you how."

"Me? Make coffee?"

"Sure, why not?"

"I wasn't allowed in the kitchen at home."

"Why not?"

"I don't know. My parents are just insane, I guess. The kitchen was off limits. Maybe they were afraid I'd eat something. I was hungry all the time."

"Is that why you're so skinny?"

"I guess. My parents were skinny, too, like me. I thought it was normal. Our neighbors were all pretty thin."

Rosie took a sip of the scalding-hot coffee. "Yeow! That's hot!"

"Try this." Bear raised his own mug to his lips, and took a long, slurping pull of the hot liquid. "See? The air mixes with the coffee and cools it off."

Rosie tried it. "Yeah, I get it. It works. Just one problem, though—at home I would have gotten smacked for making all that noise."

"Well, you're not home now," Bear said. "And that's what I wanted to talk about."

Rosie raised her eyebrows, then lowered her eyes. She rotated her coffee mug on the tabletop, making a pretty pattern with the wet rings. Finally, she positioned the mug directly in front of her, handle ninety degrees to the right, sank down in her chair, and looked up at Bear. "Are you kicking me out already?"

"What? No! Of course not! Whatever gave you that idea?"

She took another long slurping pull from the mug. "If you don't want me here, you can just tell me."

"I'm happy that you're here," Bear assured her. "But I have to wonder about *why* you're here and what your plans are. What caused you to leave home? Do you have a destination in mind? What will you do when you get there? Don't worry if you don't have answers to all of that. I'm glad you're here, and you can stay as long as you like. I won't even try to help you if you don't want me to. But if I *am* to help you, I'll need to know you a little better. So, tell me: what's on your mind?"

Rosie didn't say anything at first. Her big, blue eyes filled with tears that welled up and ran over, down her cheeks, and splashed onto her shirt.

Bear sipped his coffee and waited patiently. She'd talk when she was ready, or else she wouldn't. Cranking on her certainly wasn't the answer.

And he was right. After a little while, Rosie wiped her face on her sleeve and straightened up in her chair. "I'm going to Old Ritual City to join the Johnsonites." She looked at Bear defiantly.

Bear took another sip of coffee but said nothing.

"My parents were killing me. You said it yourself: I looked like a skeleton. I wasn't getting nearly enough to eat. Besides, they're stupid and ignorant, and they wanted me to be stupid and ignorant just like them! Plus, that Loward's Own religion of theirs is ridiculous. It's all about how they are better than everyone else because they try to be 'uplifting' all the time. But that was only to make themselves feel superior. It made me feel sick. Plus, I was a prisoner. I wasn't allowed out of the house, ever, or even out of my room, except for mealtimes and church. And school. I didn't have any friends, and if I even thought about talking to a boy, my dad would come unglued, screaming, shouting, accusing, breaking stuff. It was scary."

"When did you have a chance to talk to a boy?" Bear asked.

"Church. And there was our little school—we met together a couple of times a month. School was okay. We mostly sat in a circle and talked about our lessons, then got new assignments. Church was weird, though. There were candles, and everyone was naked, or nearly naked. And they talked in languages I didn't understand—I'm not sure if they were actual languages at all. I really didn't get what was going on. I never thought much about it, anyway—it was always like that, as far back as I can remember."

"So… you're looking for something that makes more sense?"

"Yeah. I heard about the Johnsonites from a couple of the kids at school, during break time."

"The boys you weren't supposed to be talking with?"

Rosie grinned. "Yup, those ones. I don't see anything wrong with talking to boys. Some of them are kind of cute."

"I'll bet they are," Bear said. "Anyway, I was a boy once. And now you're talking to me. Do you think I'm cute?"

"I like talking to you. And anyway, you're not a boy, you're an old man. Really old. And, yeah, you're kind of cute. I guess." She blushed furiously.

Bear laughed kindly. "I enjoy talking to you, too. It's been a while since I talked to anyone at all, except Scavs and Johnson's Militia and a few merchants. And there's a guard at the mall I talk to sometimes. And most of them don't really talk very much."

Rosie frowned. "You talk to Scavs *and* Militia? What about the Fury?"

"The Scavs and the Militia come here if they need medical treatment. I was a doctor before the War, and during the War, I was a combat medic. Do you know what that is? A combat medic is a special kind of doctor who takes care of wounded soldiers. So, when they get hurt, the Scavs and Militia come to me. I haven't seen the Furies until last night. They're fairly new. Before them, there were the Loward's Angels. I'd see them from time to time, but they weren't any trouble."

"Scavs and Militia at the same time?" Rosie asked. "Don't they fight?"

"Not here, they don't, not if they want treatment. I've made the rules very clear: there is to be no fighting here. Also, treatment isn't free. They are required to bring me what they can, when they can. That's how I get fresh onions and other fruits and vegetables, like those apples we had for breakfast. Plus, I have a garden."

"What if they don't have anything to trade? When they come to get fixed up, I mean."

"It doesn't work like that, exactly. They bring me things when they have them. Then, when they're hurt, I fix them up without asking for anything at that particular moment."

"Do they ever attack you?"

"Not anymore. They used to try, a long time ago. Every once in a while a group would show up with raiding on their minds."

"What did you do then?"

"I buried them out in the ball field, near where you came in."

"You *killed* them?"

"What did you expect me to do, give them all big bear hugs? Anyway, word got around, and pretty soon they quit trying. For a long time, now, they've come in peace, bearing gifts, and I treat them when they need it. It's better this way."

Rosie said nothing for a long time. At length, she said, "I think I understand. I just never thought about it before. It seems kind of weird that you treat Scavs and the Johnson's Militia, both."

"But I don't, though, you see. I treat wounded *people*, and I don't ask about their religions or their politics. I'm a healer, not a philosopher."

"What's a philosopher?"

"Someone who thinks too much," Bear said.

"Which are worse, Johnson's Militia or the Scavs?"

"They're about the same," Bear said. "The Militia think they are better than the Scavs because Johnson himself commissions them. They're trying to make the world a better place. Or so they say. They're supposed to stop the Scavs from preying on others, but that easily becomes an excuse for unrestrained violence. I suppose some of them mean well, but a lot of them are only human." Bear finished his coffee, then refilled his mug and topped off Rosie's.

"Tell you what," Bear said. "How about you hop up on the examination table and let me check your stitches? We want to be sure there's no infection setting in."

The Bear and The Rose

— Chapter 5 —

PARTHENOGENESIS

"Okay. Just let me go to the bathroom first." When she got back, Rosie obligingly hopped up on the table and lay down. Bear raised her shirt above her waist, removed the bandages, and examined the stitches. There was no sign of infection and only mild inflammation. So far, so good. The penicillin was doing its job.

She was amazingly thin. So thin, in fact, that she almost looked like a bare skeleton. Her ribs stuck out so far that he could count them all. She looked like the pictures he'd seen, a lifetime ago when he was still in medical school, of the prisoners-of-war in World War II, suffering from beri beri. Actually, it was more like starving kids in Botswana or wherever, the ones with the flies in their eyes that had kwashiorkor or whatever starvation disease made their little bellies stick out. Just like Rosie's. Well, that's not a problem, he thought—a few more cheeseburgers will set that right.

And then there were those scars on her arms and thighs. Most of them had healed into fine white lines, barely noticeable. But a few of them were recent, maybe two weeks old or so. He'd seen that before, too, the cutting, long ago in another time. Self-harm. A sign of a kid in distress, maybe even being abused. He frowned. Bear didn't like the idea of kids being abused. He wondered if it was connected to her parents' bizarre religion.

Then a thought occurred to him. "Would you mind if I felt your tummy?"

"Okay with me."

Bear undid Rosie's belt and loosened her jeans. He pulled them down a couple of inches, then pressed her abdomen, just above the pubic bone. Sure enough, there was the top of the uterus, just rising above the bone. Well, that explained that! It wasn't starvation at all—the girl was pregnant. Bear wondered if she knew.

He gave her another shot of penicillin, then said, "All right, all done. You can hop down now. Let's finish up our coffee and chat about a few more things."

After they sat down again, Bear filled their cups and asked, "Did your parents ever tell you about human reproduction?"

"Human repro—you mean babies?"

"I mean how babies are made."

"Well, that wasn't something we were allowed to talk about. But one time, when my dad was at work, my mom told me some stuff. It was after I started changing—you know, growing these and getting hair down there and stuff."

"What did she tell you?"

Rosie frowned. "Well, she said that when a boy and girl get married, he puts his thing, you know—"

"I know," Bear said. "I was married once, a very long time ago. Did you ever do that with a boy?"

"Of course not! I'm way too young to get married. Why are you asking me this? I'm only fourteen. Didn't I tell you that?"

"Yes, you mentioned that. This morning, when we were talking about the high school."

"Oh, right. Do I look really young? I guess I'm pretty skinny."

"Yes, you are. A few more cheeseburgers will fix that up, though."

"I thought we were going to have pizza?"

"We are. Pizza works, too."

"Oh, good. Can I help cook?"

"Of course. Anyway, I noticed that even with all your bones showing—I could count your ribs—I noticed your tummy was bulging way out. And then I thought that could be a sign of being pregnant."

"Pregnant! How in the world could I be pregnant?"

"That's an excellent question, which I can't answer right now. But if you *are* pregnant, there are some special things you'll need to do."

"Special things? Like what?"

"Well, some special foods, and there will be some special clothes. Also, some special knowledge that mothers-to-be need to know."

"Special knowledge… how will I get that? Will you teach me, Mr. The Bear? You said you were a doctor, so you must know, right?"

"Of course, I'll teach you, if that's what you need. If you want me to, that is."

"Yes, I do want! I want you to teach me everything."

Bear sighed. "Well, okay. First thing we need to do is find out if you've really got a baby in there."

"How are we going to do that?"

"Before the War, people didn't always wait until they were married to have sex."

"Sex? You mean when the boy puts his—"

"Right. That's called 'having sex'. Sometimes even people your age had sex, and sometimes they got pregnant."

"Even when they were my age?"

"Yes, sometimes even when they were your age. Back then, like now, for many kids, it wasn't something they could talk to their parents about, so the school nurse kept pregnancy tests on hand."

"What's a pregnancy test?"

"There are, or were, several kinds, but they all worked pretty much the same way. When a woman is pregnant, the chemicals in her body change, and that change can be detected in her urine."

"Urine?"

"Pee."

"Oh. I have to pee to find out?"

"Right. You pee on the little test strip and wait a minute or three. Then it'll tell you if you're pregnant or not."

Bear rummaged through the various cabinets and drawers until he found a package of pregnancy tests. "These are pretty old. They're from before the War. But they're likely still accurate, for a positive reading, anyway. We can try it several times to make sure. And there are some other ways to tell, too."

"What other ways?"

"Let's get this one done first, shall we?"

"Okay. What do I do?"

"You take this test strip with you into the restroom, then you pee on it. Make sure the entire end gets peed on, okay? Then clean yourself up and come show it to me."

Rosie frowned at the unfamiliar device, then shrugged and headed for the restroom. In a few moments she was back, and they waited together for a very long three minutes.

The test was positive.

"Does that mean I'm pregnant?"

"Yes, if the test is accurate. Remember, these are pretty old. Maybe try another one?"

Rosie took another one to the restroom, then returned.

"Positive again," Bear observed, after the three minutes were up. "Want to try a third time?"

"Not really. What are some of the other ways to tell?"

"Depends on how long you've been pregnant. Some women have morning sickness early in the pregnancy."

"What's morning sickness?"

"You throw up in the mornings."

"Uh-oh."

"What? Did you throw up?"

"Remember when I went to the bathroom before? I didn't tell you because I was afraid you'd think I was disrespecting your omelet. It was really delicious, you know—I didn't mean to puke it up."

Bear smiled a little. "It's okay, Rosie—I don't get mad about stuff like that. Still, though, it *is* one sign of pregnancy early on."

"What else?"

"When did you have your last period?"

"Period?"

"You know, the monthly bleeding down there." Bear pointed.

Rosie looked horrified. "I've never bled down there!"

"Never?"

"Never! Why would I?"

Bear shook his head. "It's a girl thing. I'll explain more about it later. Your school program or home school or whatever you were doing hasn't been working out for you, has it?"

"They never said anything about bleeding. Or having sex. Or babies."

"What *did* you learn about?"

"We learned to read, so we could read the Word of the Loward. I didn't like reading much—it was boring."

"There was a saying before the War," Bear said, "that if we taught our kids to eat ice cream the way we taught them to read, they wouldn't like ice cream, either."

"What's ice cream?"

"Something you eat after pizza."

"Oh. We learned to write, too. That was hard. I got a bump on this finger from squeezing the pencil. See?" She held up her middle finger for Bear's inspection. "We practiced doing something called maths, with numbers and stuff. I wasn't good at it. It was confusing. We read the Holy Book of the Loward."

"The Bible?"

"No, that's the old book. We read the new Book of the Loward, written by the Loward himself. Or so they said. I believed them at first, but later on, I wasn't so sure. Some of the stuff in it is kind of weird."

"I'll bet."

"There wasn't anything in it about having sex or babies. No one said anything, but we got the idea that it wasn't really 'uplifting' to talk about such things."

"How many people do you know?" Bear asked.

"What? What do you mean?"

"I mean, think of everyone you ever met. How many people is that?"

"Um… well, let's see." Rosie started counting on her fingers. "My mother and father, that's two. And you, three. People at church… maybe twenty-five or thirty. Teacher, kids at school, the neighbors, another twenty or thirty. Maybe sixty? Seventy?"

"That you know personally. How many others can you think of?"

"Other people in the whole world?"

"Yes."

"Scavs—I've seen a few gangs and heard of others. The Loward's Fury, the same. There's Johnson, in the old Downtown, and his followers and his Militia. I don't know how many followers he has. Maybe a few hundred, more or less."

"Would you believe thousands? And that's just in the Big Valley. There are millions more people all around the world that you've never met or even heard of."

"That's hard to imagine."

"Nevertheless, it's true. Before the War, there were ten billion or more."

"How many is a billion?"

"A thousand million. Or, a thousand-thousand-thousand."

"I… I… it's not that I don't believe you," Rosie said, "but I just can't picture that many people."

"It's true, though. I was there, remember, before the War, and I saw them. A lot of them, anyway. So many people that it was hard to walk down the sidewalks. So many cars on the road that it was hard to find a place to drive. But here's the thing: all the people? Everyone you know, everyone you don't know, all the people who died in the War, they all came to be because people had sex and then had babies."

Rosie's eyes grew wide, but she said nothing.

"So, what do you think? Are sex and babies something we shouldn't talk about or think about? Before the War, sometimes it seemed that sex was all anyone *ever* talked about. So why do you think your Loward says it's not uplifting to talk about sex?"

"I can't begin to guess," Rosie said. She thought hard. "Maybe something bad happened to him, and he got broken about sex."

"Yeah, maybe," Bear said. "That's a pretty good guess, Rosie."

"Well, I'm not broken about sex. I want to know everything. What are other signs of being pregnant?"

"Some women's breasts get tender, because of hormone chang- es."

Rosie tentatively tested her breasts, wincing. "Ow. Yeah, ten- der. What else?"

"When I felt your abdomen, I could feel the top of your uterus. It's definitely enlarged."

"What's a uterus?"

"It's a special organ that only females have. It's where the baby grows until it's ready to come out."

"Oh. Wait—come out? Come out where?"

"That can wait for later," Bear said. "First we'll find you some books with really good pictures in it." He raised a pedantic forefinger and intoned, "All shall become clear, my dear, all shall become clear."

Rosie laughed at Bear's antics, then grew serious again. "Are there other signs?"

"Sure. Your nipples may get darker. You may get a dark line that runs down from your belly button. But there's one sign you can't miss: in a few months, your belly will get really big. And then you'll know for sure."

"I still don't get how I got a baby in there. Like I told you, I've never… had sex… with a boy. Or anyone. Are there some other ways to get pregnant?"

"Well, yes, but they are much less common. Wait—you did mention some ceremonies at your parents' church? You were naked, you said?"

"They made me get undressed. I didn't really want to, because of all the other people, but like I told you last night, I was never allowed to be body shy. Then they put me up on a table and covered my eyes."

"And then what happened?"

"I'm not sure. There was some chanting, and I got touched all over by a lot of people. Then they let me up and I got dressed and we went home."

"Touched all over? Down there, too?" Bear nodded toward her pubic area.

"Everywhere. Could that have done it?"

"Maybe. It's not common, but it's not unheard of, either. Depends on what they touched before they touched you."

"Oh." Rosie mulled things over for a while. "Well, I don't mind having a baby, I guess. I always hoped I'd have babies someday. I just thought I'd be older."

"It happens," Bear said sympathetically.

"I'll be a wonderful mom," Rosie said. "I'll tell her everything she wants to know, whatever it is. And I'll let her talk to boys and anyone else she wants to. And I won't make her stay in her room." She thought some more, then looked up at Bear with adoring eyes. "And you're going to make a great dad, too!"

THE BEAR AND THE ROSE

— Chapter 6 —
Teacher

When Bear could breathe again, he asked Rosie gently, "Whatever gives you the idea that I'm going to be the dad?"

"Well… I don't know. It just seems… right, somehow."

"Not to me, it doesn't! I've already been a dad." He frowned and searched her eyes. "I'm really old, you know."

"You are? How old are you? Where are your children? Are they boys or girls? Why don't they live with you?"

"I'm really old. Really, *really* old. I turned sixty-one not too long ago."

"Sixty-one! That *is* old. My father is only thirty-four. You're almost twice as old as that."

"That's right, Rosie. I'm almost twice his age, and he's been a father for fourteen years already. You're almost grown up. Do you have siblings?"

"What's a sibling?"

"A brother or a sister."

"No, just me. My mother doesn't like… having sex."

"I'll bet."

"She says it's icky."

"Uh-huh."

"They don't say 'having sex,' though."

"What do they call it?"

"Well, my mother calls it 'marital dues.' My father doesn't call it anything. He never talks about it at all."

"I'm not surprised."

"So, what happened to your wife and your children?"

Bear sighed. *If I must, I must.* "Come on, I'll show you."

"Show me? They're here?"

"Just come on."

They left the nurse's office and headed back toward the cafeteria. But just as they got to a pretty stretch of grass, Bear turned and led Rosie into a little clearing between two trees. There were four stones set into the grass. They read "Amaranth, Beloved Wife and Mother," "David," "Greta," and "Carol."

Bear stood in front of the stone marked "Amaranth," hands clasped in front of him, head bowed. Bruno and Molly lay down by Amaranth's grave. Molly whined once, quietly.

Rosie read each stone carefully, then went to stand beside Bear. She took one of his hands in both of her own and stood with him, her head also bowed. After a long time, Bear took a deep breath and raised his head. "So, you want to see the library?" His voice was hoarse. "It's not really time for lunch yet."

Rosie squeezed his hand tight, then put her wispy arms around his fur coat and hugged him hard, while Bear stroked her blond hair tenderly. "Sure, I'd love that," she said, barely aloud.

As they walked along, headed for the old school library, Rosie asked, "What will we have for lunch? Another miracle food?"

"Absolutely," Bear said. "Ham and cheese sandwiches."

"I know what sandwiches are," Rosie said. "They're evil old women who live on the beach and cast spells on unsuspecting swimmers."

Bear laughed out loud. "Exactly right! Where did you learn about them?"

"Oh, in a book I read a long time ago. I got it from a girl in Church. She sneaked it in under her shirt, tucked in her waistband. During prayers, it somehow found its way under my waistband. I read it over and over until I got caught."

"Then what happened?"

"My father whipped me with his belt. Worst whipping I ever got. He said that everything we need to read is already written in the Book of the Loward."

"Big reader, your father?"

Rosie laughed. It was a pleasant sound, as if someone had rung a crystal bell. "Not so much. He has a reading disability. Something called… dis… dyslex…"

"Dyslexia?"

"Yeah, that's it. He says the letters move around and get mixed up. He's basically illiterate."

"Right. How about your mother?"

"She says she's too tired. The pills make her sleepy and she can't concentrate."

"The pills."

"They're supposed to keep her calm and happy, but mostly they just make her stupid. She used to want a better life for herself and for me, and that made my father angry, and they fought all the time. So dad got her these pills."

"I see. Is she happy now?"

"Happy? Not really. She's more like… well, she just doesn't care anymore. That's not right—I know she still cares. It's more like when you knock on your neighbor's door and there's no one home." Rosie frowned to herself, then nodded slightly. "Yes, that's right, like she's not home anymore. When I started to grow up, you know, get these"—she cupped her tiny breasts—"Dad started giving me pills, too. I didn't take them, though. I pretended to take them, then I saved them in a little envelope in my underwear drawer. When I was ready to leave, I smooshed them all up and put them in my parents' night-time herbal tea. They were asleep in just a few moments. That's when I left, thirteen days ago."

"That's why you left? Because your dad wanted to give you pills?"

"Right. Well, that and they were trying to starve me to death like I told you before. And that thing about undressing in church—I didn't like that at all. You know, the Loward's will, and all that."

"I think I'm starting to get the picture," Bear said. "A little bit, anyway. You mentioned that your idea was to head for the Old Downtown and join the Johnsonites. Is that still something you want to do, knowing that you're most likely pregnant?"

"I… I don't know? What do you think I should do?"

"Hold on, now—I'm not in the business of being your boss. This is a decision you have to make for yourself. Isn't that why you left home? So you could be your own boss?"

Rosie scowled. "Well, yes, but… this is hard! When I left, I didn't know I was pregnant."

"Now that you know, do you wish you had stayed home? I could take you back."

"Oh, no, absolutely not! I'm ten times happier than when I left. Diablo is no place for having babies!"

"Fair enough. But—if you're going to be on your own, you're going to have to learn how to evaluate your options and make executive decisions."

"Okay. I can do that! Will you teach me how, Mr. The Bear?"

Bear smacked his forehead. *How did I get myself into this? I could have just sent her on her way this morning with my good wishes. Not really,* he admonished himself. *When have you ever abandoned a pregnant woman or a small child? And this one is as ignorant and inexperienced as they come. You know you'd be sending her to certain death.*

Bear sighed a long, shuddering sigh. "All right, Rosie. But on one condition: you'll have to pay close attention and think very hard, even when your brain is tired. And no complaining. I hate complaining."

"I will, Mr. The Bear. I promise. I'll study as hard as I know how."

"All right, then. Here's an example: have you given any thought to where you will live or how you'll find food?"

Rosie blushed. "No, not really. My main idea was just to get away from Diablo and my parents. Which I did, you know."

"Yeah, I know. And how did that work out for you?"

She hung her head. "Cold, wet, and hungry."

"And wounded. And pregnant."

"I must have been pregnant *before* I left Diablo."

"Fair point. Still, now you have both yourself and a baby to think about and few, if any, real-world skills. How do you think that baby will get the food that it needs to grow inside you?"

"I don't know. That kind of talk wasn't considered—"

"—uplifting. Yeah, I get the picture. But that's the past, this is now. For now, you're going to need a new set of values. Try this on: all knowledge is uplifting, but ignorance is a disaster."

"All knowledge is uplifting." Rosie mulled that over. "That's a change, all right. It'll take some getting used to. But I like it. I hated not knowing about anything, especially about how stuff works."

"The study of How Things Work is called 'Science.'"

"The Book of the Loward says that Science is a tool of the devil. Is it?"

They had arrived at the administration wing, but instead of going inside, Bear sat on a bench in the courtyard between the administration offices and the school library. He patted the bench, inviting Rosie to join him.

"What do you think?" Bear asked. "If you're going to use your own mind, you'll have to figure stuff like that out for yourself."

Rosie thought hard as she watched Bruno and Molly happily sniffing at every pillar and post as though they'd never been there before. Bruno was making sure that any other dog who might come this way would know that it was Bruno's territory.

"He's going to be awfully thirsty by the time he's done," Rosie observed.

"He's thirsty now," Bear said. He took a key ring from his pocket and used a key to open the valve of a nearby hose bib. Both dogs lapped greedily at the stream of water.

Bear returned to the bench. "Well, what did you think of? Did you draw a conclusion?"

"Maybe. The Book of the Loward says that the Loward made all things. Well, if He did, then He knows how everything works, right? That would make Him the greatest scientist that ever lived."

"Logical enough," Bear said, neither agreeing nor disagreeing in tone or facial expression. "Then why would the Book of the Loward say that Science is from the devil?"

Rosie laughed. "That's an easy question. It's because it's full of—"

"Okay, okay," Bear said. "Also a logical conclusion."

"I may be ignorant, Mr. The Bear, but I'm not stupid. And I'm not going to be ignorant for long!"

"Indeed you are not stupid, Rosie. And a good thing, too, because you're going to need all the smarts you can muster to take care of yourself and your baby in this world. I'll help you, but not forever. I'm old now, and getting older fast. The time will come when you'll have to think and do for yourself."

Rosie's eyes filled with tears. "Don't die too soon, please. I need to know what you know. I need a teacher."

Bear smiled and patted her shoulder. "Not quite, kid. It took me a lifetime to learn what I know. Several lifetimes, really. What you need is to learn how to teach yourself. Try this on: 'you don't have to know everything, you just have to know how to find out.'

It's something my father used to tell me when I was your age. Get it?"

Rosie thought that over. "I get it, I think. My lifetime will be different from yours, right? *Very* different. For example, the War. You went through it, I didn't. And you were married, and had a wife, and kids, and I'm having a baby without a husband and I never even had sex. Different lives need different knowledge." She took a long, slow, deep breath. "Was she pretty?"

"What? Who?"

"Your wife. Am… Ama…"

"Amaranth. It means a kind of plant with beautiful flowers. You could eat the seeds. Yes, she was beautiful. I have a picture—I'll show you." He laughed. "Another name for amaranth was 'pigweed.' When she got mad at me, I called her Pigweed. That always made her laugh, and it's hard to stay mad when you're laughing. We never stayed mad at each other for long."

"Not ever?"

"Not ever."

"That's sweet. I wish I had known her."

"You would have loved her, Rosie," Bear said sadly. "Everybody did." He shook off his melancholy. "If you want to know how to find out everything you'll ever need to know, one great place to start is the library. Are you ready to have a look?"

"Oh, yes, please!"

— Chapter 7 —

Library

WHEN THEY GOT inside, Rosie stopped and stared, slack-jawed. "Books," she whispered. "Millions and millions of them."

"Thousands, anyway," Bear agreed.

"Can… *may*… I touch them?"

"Of course," Bear said. "They're not holy books, or sacred in any way. Although you can find several copies of the real Christian Bible in here, what your people call the Old Bible. Also, the holy books of some other religions. But mostly they are just ordinary books."

Rosie walked among the shelves, letting her fingertips drift along the spines of hundreds of dusty tomes. "So many," she whispered. "Have you read them all, Mr. The Bear?"

"Nearly all," Bear said. "I've been alone here for a very long time. Since just before the War, you know."

"How long ago is that, exactly?"

"Well, let me see now. Umm… thirty-four… no, thirty-five years. Yeah, that's right, thirty-five."

"That's more than twice as long as I've been alive."

"I suppose that's true," Bear said, frowning.

"That's very difficult to imagine. I feel like I've always been alive, that nothing real happened before I was born."

"Everybody feels like that," Bear reassured her. "It's normal. Just like you can't really imagine what the world will be like after you're dead. I think about it sometimes—I'm a lot closer to old age than I am to my youth, nowadays."

Rosie looked like she was going to cry again. To distract her from that line of thought, Bear said, "You know, Rosie Girl, there are basically three kinds of books in most libraries."

Rosie ran her sleeve across her eyes. "Three kinds?"

"Right. You can see the signs: over there is Fiction. You know what that is?"

"Not really. The Book of the Loward says—"

"I can imagine. Fiction means that the stories are made up. They didn't really happen. The writers sometimes based the stories on things that did happen, or even things that might have happened, but they didn't actually happen."

"Lies, you mean?"

"Not at all. People tell lies to deceive other people. But people tell stories for lots of reasons: to inspire, to educate, to illustrate something, or to make a point. Or even just to entertain. It's fun, but it can also be educational. Some stories help us figure out who we are, and who we want to become."

Rosie's brow furrowed. "I don't understand."

"Doesn't the Book of the Loward have something called 'parables'?"

"Well, yes, but—"

"Are the parables true stories?"

"Well, no, but—"

"There you are, then. Don't worry about it. After you read a few dozen books, you'll get the idea."

"I'm going to read these books?"

"If you want me to be your teacher, you are. It's part of the course. You might even like it."

Rosie looked doubtful, but said nothing.

"Over there," Bear continued, "are the Non-Fiction books. Want to take a guess?"

"Well, if fiction is made-up stuff, then non-fiction must be true stuff."

"Precisely!" Bear beamed. "Good work! Smart girl! You can find entire books about all kinds of things. For example, when I started my garden I found a book on gardening. It taught me how to prepare the soil, how to plant seeds, and how to harvest. Another book taught me how to store food so it doesn't spoil."

"Is there a book about having babies, or having sex?"

"I don't know," Bear said. "I never looked—never came up— I've been here alone a long time. No sex, no babies. There are several about training dogs, though."

"I'm probably not having puppies," Rosie said soberly, then grinned up at Bear.

Bear grinned back. "Probably not. The problem is that even before the War, there were plenty of people who felt that having sex and having babies weren't appropriate subjects for high-school students. Not everyone agreed, though. We'll have to poke around the shelves."

Rosie said, "Wait a minute. Are you telling me that this place once held a couple of thousand teenagers, boys and girls together, and people thought they shouldn't know about sex? Were they crazy back then, or just plain stupid?"

Bear smiled sadly. "I've asked myself that same question. A little of both, I suppose. The kids had sex anyway, though, many of them, often without knowing how to prevent unwanted pregnancies. That's why there are pregnancy tests in the school nurse's office."

"I don't get it," Rosie grumbled. "It makes no sense to me."

"Rosie, think about it for a moment. If the pre-War people were sensible, do you think there would even have been a war?"

"Oh." Rosie shook her head. "I thought it was just the followers of the Loward."

"'Fraid not, Rosie Girl. People have been senseless and mean as long as there have been people. There are entire books about that, too. You'll find them in Non-Fiction. But you don't want to start with the depressing stuff." He shook off his melancholy and went to the Fiction section. He rummaged around the shelves, selected a book, and handed it to her. "Here, try this one."

In the cover illustration, a man dressed in a bright green suit with a funny-shaped matching green hat drew a very long bow, while a man in a brown suit looked on. "'The Merry Adventures of Robin Hood by Howard Pyle,'" Rosie read carefully. "Not the sort of thing my parents would approve." She took a pedantic tone. "Shooting people with a bow isn't 'uplifting', you know."

"Doesn't that rather depend on who's getting shot?" Bear asked. "And why?"

Rosie laughed. "You know, I never thought of that. Yes, of course it does." She handed the book to Bear.

"Take it with you," Bear said. "You can put it on the table by your bedside, and read it before you go to sleep. For now, though, go ahead and explore the library. Ask me about anything interesting you might find."

Rosie headed straight for the non-fiction section to search for books about having babies. But before she had a chance to find anything, Bruno and Molly leaped to their feet, legs stiff, heads low, and growled in the direction of the door.

— Chapter 8 —

Visitors

"Come on!" Bear grabbed Rosie's arm and hauled her out of the library toward the administration building.

"Ow! Hey! What's going on?"

"Quiet now. Get inside. Follow me."

Rosie thought they were going to the nurse's office again, but instead, Bear turned into what was once the school principal's office. He opened a closet that wasn't a closet at all, but a narrow flight of stairs leading to a fortified structure on the roof, affording a clear, unobstructed view of the parking lot.

Rosie followed Bear up the stairs and looked for a light switch, but Bear slapped her hand away. "Leave it!"

He opened a locked cabinet and removed two double-barreled shotguns, a long sniper rifle with a huge scope, and a .45 automatic pistol. He checked each one for ammunition, then set the shotguns aside, put the pistol in his waistband, and positioned the sniper rifle in a narrow vertical window cut into the steel wall.

"Hush now, be still. Listen."

"I don't hear anything."

Bear growled, "Well, stop talking and listen until you do." He turned to the dogs, who were moving about restlessly and whining. "You, too," he snapped. The dogs subsided.

From far away came the staccato sound of ragged gunfire, accompanied by the sound of an overtaxed internal combustion engine. A white panel van came roaring up the street and turned into the high-school parking lot. It screeched to a halt just below Bear's defensive position. Several dozen bullet holes perforated the rear of the van's body.

In the distance, a dark-colored military-looking vehicle approached, still firing at the van. "Stay inside the vehicle," Bear yelled. "Keep your heads down."

He peered through the scope of the sniper rifle, drew a bead on the incoming military vehicle, and squeezed the trigger. Nothing seemed to happen, at first, but after a moment, the attacking vehicle appeared to slow down.

Bear repeated the process, squeezed off another shot. This time, the vehicle swerved to the side of the road, where it paused, then spun around and roared off in the direction from which it came.

Bear waited for what seemed to Rosie a long time, but the vehicle didn't reappear. There was no sign of movement from the white van. Bear called down, "Okay, you can open the door, but stay inside. Identify yourselves. Turn on the inside light and let me see you."

The van's side door slid open. A voice called up. "Bear! It's me, Rat. I'm with Echo and JR. We've got a new guy with us, name of Jimmy. Echo's been wounded."

"All right, then, I'll come down," Bear said. "Best if you stay in the van until I get there."

"Sure thing, Bear," Jimmy said. "But hurry—Echo's bleeding all over the place."

Bear looked up and down the street in front of the school. There was no sign of movement. Rosie and the dogs followed Bear back to the bottom of the stairs. Bear pointed to the high-backed chair behind the principal's desk. "Sit there. Stay there until I come get you. Understand?"

Rosie nodded. "I'm staying right here."

Bear exited to the courtyard and unchained the door to the parking lot. He checked the street again, then waved at Rat. "Okay, come on in. Quickly now. Nurse's office, you know where it is."

The three boys half-dragged, half-carried the now-unconscious Echo to the nurse's station and hoisted her onto the examination table.

"What's her problem?" Bear asked.

"Leg wound, upper right thigh," Rat said.

"Get her pants off. Let's have a look."

The three boys looked at each other uncomfortably, then Rat tentatively undid the snap of her jeans, pulled the zipper down, then stopped awkwardly.

"For the love of Pete!" Bear growled. He undid the girl's zipper, pulled her pants off, and examined the wound. "It's only a scratch. Bullet just grazed her thigh."

"The bullets were coming right through the van walls," Rat said.

"I don't doubt it," Bear said. "Those guys looked like Loward's Fury, the new group. How did they find you?"

"We were scavenging in some old houses north of the Mall," Rat explained.

"Mostly flattened," JR added in his quiet, gentle voice.

"Yeah, mostly," Rat agreed. "But pickings are getting slim everywhere, so we figured we'd give it a try. We were in this one house, a couple of rooms were still standing, poking in all the dark corners, you know. When we went back outside, that army truck, or whatever it was, was coming up the street. They started shooting without warning, so we jumped into the van and took off as fast as we could go."

"Which was pretty fast," JR said. "We didn't waste any time, that's for sure."

"I'm sorry we involved you, Bear," Rat said. "You were the closest place we could think of."

"No worries," Bear said. "I'm always prepared for such an occurrence, though we haven't had one for a good long time."

"Except for last night," Rosie said quietly from the doorway of the principal's office.

"Whoa ho! Who's this?" Jimmy leered at Rosie. "Looks like Bear's got a girl toy!"

Rat backhanded Jimmy viciously across the face. "Shut up, Jimmy."

"I thought I told you to stay put!" Bear growled at Rosie.

"I did," Rosie said, "for a while. But I came when I heard voices."

"I'll just bet you did," mumbled Jimmy, through the blood trickling down his face.

Rat hauled back to smack Jimmy again, but Bear caught his hand. "Enough! This is the nurse's office—neutral territory. Show some respect. You gotta discipline your crew, your business. But take it outside, okay? Also, in case you haven't noticed, I'm in the middle of patching up Echo."

"Of course," Rat said. "Sorry, Bear. My bad."

"As for you," Bear roared at Jimmy, "one more nasty crack from you and you're banned for life, what little of it you might have left. I won't have that kind of lewd talk. Not ever, understood?"

Jimmy nodded, but his stormy expression said he didn't like it one bit.

To everyone, Bear said in his normal voice, "This is Rosie. That's 'Miss Rose' to you fellows. She came to me last night, in the middle of the night. The Loward's Fury, maybe even that same group, caught up with her and threatened rape, murder, and returning her to her parents. She got in through the hedge, I still don't know how, which is when I found her. She had a bad wound in her abdomen that required stitching. If I hadn't found her, she'd be dead now."

"Loward's Fury again," Rat said thoughtfully. "We never used to see them this far out. Neighborhood's going to the dogs."

Bruno's ears pricked, and he growled softly.

"No offense, Bruno," Rat said, and scratched Bruno's ears.

"Now listen carefully, all of you. Especially you, Jimmy. Rosie is under my protection. Do you all understand what that means?"

"Yes, Bear," Rat said.

"Yes, Bear," JR echoed.

"Jimmy?" Bear prompted.

"Yeah," Jimmy grunted sullenly. "Whatever."

Bear reached out and grabbed Jimmy with his ham-sized fist, then dragged Jimmy's face up to within an inch of his own. Bruno and Molly leaped to their feet and growled at Jimmy, teeth bared, eyes bright. "Don't you 'whatever' me, you young punk. I'm sure we can find room for you in the ball field. Do I need to take you there right now?"

Jimmy's eyes bulged. "No, Bear. I… I'm sorry. I apologize. I'm just in a bad mood, is all, I guess."

"Well, don't bring it in here, ever again! Understand me?"

"Yes, Bear."

Bear released his grip. Jimmy sagged down into one of the armchairs along the wall, but his eyes burned like hot coals.

"Now, then," Bear said. "Do you think we can take care of this girl now? First thing we need to do is clean the wound. Rosie, do you want to learn how to do this? Might come in handy someday."

Rosie approached the examination table and took the spot directly across from Bear. Rat and JR politely made space for her. "What do I do?"

Bear opened a paper packet of sterile cotton wool and gave it to Rosie, along with a bottle of rubbing alcohol. "Wet the cotton with the alcohol. Clean the wound thoroughly. Here, JR, hold this flashlight for her. You have to get every bit of dirt and debris out of the wound, or it could cause an infection, which could kill Echo. I'll get some bandages."

Rosie tentatively dabbed at the wound. Echo twitched when the alcohol made contact, and Rosie jumped back a little. "I'm hurting her."

"Ignore it," Bear instructed. "It's just reflex. Echo can't feel much of anything, because she's unconscious. Don't worry about hurting her, just dig in and get the wound clean."

"Right," said Rosie. She straightened up, took a deep breath, put her fear and anxiety aside, then dug in boldly. She carefully cleaned the wound, making sure that not a single speck of foreign matter remained. "Okay, Mr. The Bear. I think it's your turn."

Bear examined the wound, then turned to Rosie with a surprised look. "This is a very fine job. You did well for your first time. This *is* your first time, right?"

"Yes, except for minor kid stuff, like splinters and scrapes. And even then it was my mother's job, really, not mine."

Bear showed Rosie how to apply a bandage. "Not too tight around the leg," Bear said. "There's an important artery that runs close to those wounds. We don't want to restrict blood flow. In fact, if that wound had been much deeper, little Echo here might have bled out in a very short time. Minutes, only."

"You mean," JR asked timidly, "she could have died?"

"That's exactly what I mean. I've seen it happen, you know."

"In the War?" JR asked. "Um… Rat said you were in the big war, the, uh, War of Righteousness."

"I was in the big war," Bear said, "but I can't vouch for how righteous it was. Righteous or not, though, I can tell you that it was ugly. Really ugly. And a lot of people died." He put a blanket over Echo, who appeared to be resting comfortably. "When she wakes up, I'll give her some medication for the pain. And she's going to need a new pair of pants. I don't suppose you boys have a spare pair in that van of yours?"

They didn't.

"She can wear my spare pair," Rosie said. "We're about the same size. Close enough, anyway."

"They're still in the dryer," Bear said.

"I'll get them," Rosie said. "It'll just be a moment."

Bear was still fussing with the unconscious Echo when Rosie returned, bearing the jeans and her spare top, too. Bear set the clothes on the bedside table. "She'll find them when she wakes up." He gently lifted Echo from the examination table and placed her on one of the patient beds, then tucked the blanket around her. He settled into the armchair next to Jimmy, who was dozing. "We'll have to wait for her to wake up. It shouldn't be long. But we don't want her to wake up alone in a strange place."

Rosie found a straight-backed metal chair and dragged it to Echo's bedside. She sat down, got as comfortable as she could, and began reading *The Adventures of Robin Hood and his Merrie Men*. She'd brought it back with her when she fetched the clothes.

Bear watched her, and smiled.

— Chapter 9 —

LOGISTICS

WHEN BEAR FELT sure that Echo was going to sleep for a while, and that Rosie was okay with watching her, he got up quietly and went to the door. "Rosie, I know you were looking forward to making pizza, but it's getting late. How would you feel about staying with Echo while the boys and I whip up a batch? We'll bring you some when it's ready."

Rosie looked disappointed, but said, "I don't mind. I can learn to make pizza later. I'll be fine here."

Bear studied Rosie's face, then said, "Okay. Molly can stay with you, too. We'll be a little while, but not too long." He opened the door and gestured Rat, JR, and Jimmy out into the corridor, then gave Rosie a last inquiring look.

"It's fine," Rosie said. "I'm reading about this guy, Robin Hood, and how he got in trouble for shooting something called a hart, and then a man called a Forester. I don't understand it all, but Robin was sad because he had killed a man."

"It's a heavy thing to take any life," Bear said, "but to take a human life is the heaviest of all." He sighed deeply and looked gravely at Rosie. "Sometimes, though, life doesn't give you much of a choice. It comes down to 'kill or be killed.' I've done my share, over the years, in the War, and after, too, and I can tell you—it's not a pleasant thing."

"After the war?" Jimmy asked.

"There's a reason the gangs leave me alone."

"Hence the ball field," JR said. "You don't want to go there."

Jimmy scowled but said nothing.

"I'll be back with some chow." The door closed behind him, and he was gone into the dark corridor.

Rosie wasn't sure exactly how to feel about being left alone with the wounded Echo. On the one hand, she felt rather grown-up. She'd never really been in charge of another person before, except for her grandma when she was sick and Rosie's mom had to go out.

On the other hand, looking after grandma wasn't anything like keeping vigil over an unconscious, wounded girl her own age. What if Echo woke up screaming or something bad? What would she do?

And what about these newcomers? Mr. The Bear seemed to know who they were, except maybe for Jimmy. And they acted as though they knew Bear—again, except for Jimmy. But Jimmy was getting to know Mr. The Bear pretty quickly, especially the part about the ball field. Rosie shivered.

Rosie went back to her book. It seemed that this young fellow, Robin, was only a few years older than Rosie, and that he lived away from other people, out in the woods, with his gang, The Merrie Men. He was a good bow-shooter, called an archer, and he was pretty good at fighting with a stick, too—some kind of special stick called a quarterstaff. Also, he helped people, though the book didn't say exactly how. Maybe that part came later.

Rosie wondered if Echo or any of the boys knew Johnson personally. She'd dreamed about being Johnson's wife since she was a little girl. Johnson was basically a king of sorts—well, a leader, anyway, so if Rosie married Johnson, she'd become a queen, wouldn't she? Or, at least, a Leaderess. Leaderette? Hmm. Didn't sound right. 'Queen' sounded much nicer.

Rosie wondered if having a baby already would make Johnson want her more. Lots of women, after the War, weren't able to have babies anymore. And some that did, well, the babies were… 'deformed' was the word her mother had used. Didn't live long after birth.

What if *my* baby doesn't live? She hadn't thought of that before. Her mom had said something about it in one of her endless rants—Rosie hadn't been listening much, as usual—about that's what the rituals at the Church of the Loward were all for: having healthy babies. Rosie thought about this for a bit, but couldn't see a connection between getting naked, getting touched all over, and babies not dying. Maybe Mr. The Bear could work out the connection—if there was one.

Echo stirred a little, but didn't wake up. Rosie made sure her blanket was tucked in, then felt Echo's forehead. No sign of fever. Rosie returned to Robin Hood. She was having some trouble following the second chapter, which had to do with someone called a 'tinker,' whatever that was, whose unlikely name was 'Wat o' the Crabstaff.' Maybe the writer meant 'thinker.' That, at least, made a kind of sense. Rosie couldn't make much out of the guy's name, either, except wasn't a crab some kind of sea animal? Or was it a desert animal? She couldn't remember. More stuff to ask Mr. The Bear about.

Echo moaned and tried to sit up. Rosie put Robin Hood aside and stood to look at Echo's face, now lined in pain. Echo blinked a few times, groaned again, and asked, "Who are you? Where am I? What's going on? Where's Rat? And the others? What happened?" Her questions were interrupted by a lengthy coughing episode, after which Echo fell back on her pillow and closed her eyes.

"Whoa, easy, Echo. I'll get you some water." Rosie brought a cup of water from the sink and helped Echo swallow a few mouthfuls. "I'll tell you everything I know, okay? Just take it easy."

Echo nodded and subsided.

Rosie enumerated on her fingers, just as Bear had done for her. "One: I'm Rosie. Two: you're at Mr. The Bear's place. Three: Rat and the boys and Mr. The Bear are down at the cafeteria, making something called 'pizza.' Four: you got grazed by a bullet. Mr. The Bear fixed it up for you. Five: I'm watching over you until Mr. The Bear gets back, which shouldn't be long. Okay?"

Echo's sudden smile seemed to illuminate the room. "Okay? I'll say it's okay. Bear's pizza is more than okay, it's fantastic! How long have I been here?"

"Not too long. Maybe an hour, maybe a little more. The boys brought you in. Your leg was bleeding pretty bad."

Echo lifted the sheet and peeked at her bandaged thigh. "Hey! Where are my pants? Who took my pants off? Did the boys see me without my pants? I don't *let* boys see me without my pants!"

"Easy does it, Echo," Rosie said. "Try to stay calm. Yes, I'm afraid your pants had to come off. They had a huge hole in them and were soaked with blood. They have left this world and gone to wherever old and faithful jeans go when they die."

Echo cracked up. "Okay, well, I guess it's not so bad. I still have my panties on, anyway. Not much different from a swimming suit."

"I wouldn't know about swimming suits," Rosie said, "but Mr. The Bear made the boys treat you with respect. It was strictly for medical purposes. I cleaned your wound thoroughly to prevent infection. Mr. The Bear bandaged it. The boys helped out as best they could." Rosie didn't see any point in mentioning Jimmy's behavior. "No one was rude."

"I guess they weren't, not around Bear, anyway. He doesn't go for being rude to females. Some pre-War thing, I don't know. I'm going to need some new pants, I guess. Can't wear Bear's. Well, I *could* wear Bear's pants. We all could—at the same time!"

Both girls erupted in giggles. Rosie held up the pair of pants on the bedside table. "I brought you my spare pair. We're about the same size."

Echo took the jeans from Rosie and looked them over. Her eyes brimmed with tears. "Yeah, about the same size. I'm sure they'll be fine. That's very… kind… of you." She wiped her eyes with her forearm. "Sorry, I'm not much used to kindness. I'll make it up to you, sometime, if I can. Maybe take you shopping."

"Shopping?"

"At the mall."

"What's a mall?"

"It's where a bunch of merchants sell stuff, all kinds of stuff, all in one place."

"Why wasn't it scavenged a long time ago?"

"Well, it was, and it wasn't. What happened was that a bunch of gangs got the idea to loot the place at about the same time. But it wasn't that easy."

"Why not?"

"Because of something that Rat calls 'logistics.' I think he learned it from Bear. It means 'moving stuff around.' There is, or was, a *lot* of stuff at the mall. Tons and tons of things. Bear says it's because there were thousands and thousands of people back then, before the War, you know. It's a huge place. And all around it, there are a bunch more stores that aren't actually connected, only really close, see?"

"I still don't get it. Why wasn't it looted?"

"Well, let's say you want to loot everything out of the mall. First, how are you going to move it? You'd need bunches of trucks, or a zillion people to carry it. Next, where are you going to put it all? You'd have to have another place as big as the mall to store it in, right? Then you'd have to defend it. Protect it, you see?"

"From Scavs?"

"From everybody. Scavs, Johnson's Militia, Independents, what's left of them, and that new bunch, the Loward's Fury. Also rats, bugs, rain, you name it. It made more sense just to leave it where it was, and make sure everyone got a fair share."

"Fair share? Who gets to say what's fair?"

"Good question. At first, there were a lot of fights about that, and even a few gang wars. But eventually, Johnson worked out a plan."

"Johnson?"

"Surely you've heard of Johnson? He's the leader of the Johnsonites. His capital is in Old Ritual—Old City, the old downtown."

"I've heard of him," Rosie said. "But I didn't know about a plan for the mall. Have you been there? To Old Ritual, I mean."

"Sure, lots of times."

"Have you ever seen Johnson? In person?"

"Sure. He's just a dude, like the rest of us. He's trying to help people 'improve the quality of their lives' is what he says."

"So he's not like a king or something?"

"Not really. Though he probably could be, if he wanted to. He's done a lot of good for a lot of people. There's only one thing he doesn't like."

"What's that?"

"The Loward's Own. Especially The Fury."

Rosie blushed and looked at the floor.

"What? Are you a Loward's Own?"

Rosie hesitated, then took the leap of faith. "My parents are. I… I was raised that way. That's the main reason I left home. Is that bad?"

"No! Not bad at all." Echo laughed. "You're not alone! Lots of Johnsonites were raised Loward's Own." She gave Rosie a look and a wink.

"What? You too?"

"Me too. I left home a couple of years ago. I couldn't stand the constant snotty superiority."

Rosie said nothing, but she relaxed for the first time since Echo awoke.

"Don't tell anyone, okay?" Echo said. "Not everyone gets it."

"You, too. About me, I mean. Anyway, I'm not sure *I* get it. Want me to help you get your pants on before the boys get back?"

Echo nodded, so, with some difficulty, they wriggled Rosie's spare jeans onto Echo's spare figure. They fit perfectly. And just in time, too, for the moment they were finished, the door burst open and in came Bear and the boys bearing trays of hot, steaming pizza, smelling of wonderful deliciousness!

— Chapter 10 —

Just Asking

"**D**ig in," Bear invited. "It's not nearly as good if you let it get cold."

They dug in.

Rosie thoroughly enjoyed her first experience with pizza. After she tasted it and pronounced it good, she analyzed it for completeness according to the Five Basic Food Groups she'd learned about the day before. "Crust for grains, tomato sauce for fruit. Well, it is, technically," she insisted over protests of the boys. "Some kind of unidentified meat for protein, cheese for dairy, and all kinds of little vegetables. Another perfect food for omnivores."

Soon the trays were empty, and the girls and boys were full. They sat back in their chairs, patting their bulging bellies and smiling.

"Where do you get all this food from, Mister Bear?" Jimmy asked with a tinge of suspicion in his voice.

"Shut up, Jimmy," Rat said. "Privacy, remember?"

"But I want to know," Jimmy insisted.

Rat started to get to his feet, but Bear waved him back down. "It's okay, Rat. I don't mind. It's no big secret, really. It's this way, Jimmy: I grow most of it, trade for what I can't grow. A small amount is left over from when I bought the place. No one bothered to empty the big freezer. That orange juice you guzzled is at least thirty-five years old."

Jimmy looked a little green around the gills.

Rat laughed. "What's the matter, Jimmy? It didn't seem to bother you when you were drinking it."

Jimmy flushed, then growled, "It just seems to me that Mister Bear, here, lives a lot better than most of us. He appears to have plenty of everything. What's his secret? That's what I want to know." He turned on Bear. "Well, Mister Bear, what exactly *is* your secret? Why are you living like a king while the rest of us scrounge? Who do you think you are, anyway? Maybe we'll just take our share before we go. How about that, huh?"

Rat stood up, grabbed Jimmy by the collar, and drew back his fist. But Bear gripped Rat by the shoulder and pushed him back down in the chair. "Sit tight, Rat. I said I don't mind. Jimmy here just wants to know how I do it. And I'm happy to explain it all to him." He turned his chair to face Jimmy and drew it close until his face almost touched Jimmy's. "You want to know how I do it? Well, it's like this, son. I'm smarter than you. I'm older than you. I'm more experienced than you. I think better than you do. I've read far more than you have. And I work a lot harder than you do. See?"

Jimmy's face contorted into a furious scowl. He tried to get up, but Bear was too close and sat him back down with a single look. "I don't know you, Jimmy. I only just met you. But I have to say that I don't much care for what I've seen. I've known Rat and JR for a long while, and Miss Echo, too. They work hard, like me. They're honest with me. They trade with me for services rendered. They bust their backsides scavenging, and as far as I can tell, they're making some headway. You, on the other hand, where did you come from, and what do you contribute? Or do you just schmooze along with them in the van, making eyes at Miss Echo?

Do you actually produce anything of value?" He waited, but Jimmy didn't answer. "Pah! I didn't think so," Bear said. "Just another moocher. Well, moochers don't live long in this world, Jimmy, so you'd best either straighten up or prepare for doom. And if I ever hear that you've messed with my friends"—he indicated the two boys and Echo—"I'll hunt you down and kill you, and plant you in the ball field alongside a dozen others just like you. Now, let's go."

He jerked Jimmy to his feet, frog-marched him to the main entrance accompanied by Bruno and Molly, who seem to regard the proceedings as a kind of holiday, then booted him into the parking lot. "One last thing, Jimmy—I'm also a lot meaner than you—meaner than you'll ever be. Get it? Now move out! Beat it! If you're here when I come out next, which will be in about ten minutes, I'll take care of you. Understand? Well, what are you waiting for? Hit the road!"

Bear locked the main door and chained it shut, then rejoined his friends. "I'm sorry," Bear said, "but that was about enough of that. How long has he been with you three?"

"Not long," Rat said.

"Only a few days," Echo clarified. "Don't worry—I won't miss him. He gave me the creeps."

"Me, too," JR admitted. "I didn't like the way he looked at Echo, either."

"He pawed at me some when you two weren't around," Echo said.

Rat was suddenly livid. "He *what?* You should have told me!"

Echo hung her head. "I know, Rat. You're right, I should have. I'm sorry. I was afraid there would be trouble."

"You're right about that," Rat fumed. "I'll say there would have been trouble!"

Bear took Echo's hands gently in his own. "Rat's right, you know, Miss Echo. Jimmy was trouble. But you should have told Rat. You can't let people who disrespect you be part of your little family, or they will undo all the good you've worked so hard for." He released her hands, stood up, and walked around the table. "I saw it before the War. There was, back then, an armed police force that was supposed to suppress criminals. Oh, yes, we had criminals of all sorts back then, too: looters, thieves, robbers, murderers, even"—he glanced at the girls—"rapists, men who forced women and sometimes men to have sex with them against their will. Instead of punishing them, the pre-War courts only confined them briefly, if at all, sometimes just let them go again on something called a 'technicality.' Naturally, the badness in the world got worse and worse, while the good people struggled to protect themselves. That's a big part of the reason the War of Righteousness got started in the first place—people got tired of being victimized."

He let the kids think this over, then went on, "The worst part about it is that it was completely unnecessary. Three thousand years ago, a wise king wrote these words: 'Because sentence against an evil work is not executed speedily, therefore the heart of the sons of men is fully set in them to do evil.' That old king knew that there's only one way to take care of bad people: speedily."

Rat laughed. "Well, I guess you took care of Jimmy speedily enough. He never saw it coming. Nearly made his head spin."

"Thank you for that, Bear," Echo said quietly.

"And for the lesson, too," JR added. "We needed to hear it."

"And we did hear it, Bear," Rat said quietly. "Jimmy won't happen to our family again, sir."

"I'm glad to hear it," Bear said. "Here's another saying by a leader who lived long before the king I mentioned. He spoke to the effect that 'You should not let your eye feel sorry for the evildoer, but you must put him to death so that others will see and be afraid.'"

"Are you saying we should start killing evildoers?" Echo asked. "I... I'm not sure I could do that."

"No, Echo," JR said. "Bear doesn't mean we need to start a killing spree. He's trying to show us that there's a time for killing, and when that time comes around, we have to step up right away and do what's necessary, or things will only get worse."

Rat blinked hard several times, then smiled. He put his hand on JR's shoulder. "Why, JR! That was very well said. You can certainly be eloquent when you try."

"Plus, he's absolutely right," Bear added. "I'm not advocating wholesale slaughter by any means, but sometimes people leave you very little choice. And when that time comes, prompt action is key."

Bear shook off the effects of the melancholy subject, then announced, "Okay, gang, daylight's burnin', as my dear old daddy used to say. Let's go over to the mall and see if we can get these girls some new clothes!"

Bear led the way back to the front door and unlocked it. "Okay, boys, get that van of yours warmed up and I'll meet you back here with the shopping cart." Bear looked up and down the avenue in front of the school. "Looks like Jimmy decided not to hang around. Just as well. Speaking of which, weren't you worried about someone messing with your van last night? We could have parked it around back."

Rat shrugged. "Nah, nobody messes with our van. Pretty much for the same reason nobody messes with your high school."

"Well done," Bear said. "I'll be around in a few minutes." He locked and chained the front door. "Well, how about it, Bruno? Molly? You want to go for a ride in the car? Huh? Do you?"

The dogs barked and whined and frolicked around Bear's legs. Apparently, they did.

In the same tone, he asked, "How about you, Rosie Girl? You want to go for a ride in the car?"

Rosie barked a couple of times and joined the dogs in their frolicking. Bear had to laugh. "Good girl, good Rosie!" Rosie laughed, too, and they all headed for the auto shop at the extreme north end of the old high school.

Bear opened the auto shop door and turned on the lights. The musty smell made Rosie cough, but it smelled familiar, somehow, a bit like when her father worked on mechanical things. For a moment, an overwhelming flood of nostalgia, even homesickness, nearly paralyzed her. But she shook it off and was soon distracted by the contents of the room. It seemed that this room must contain every kind of tool there ever was. But the real eye-catcher was the enormous army tank parked in the center of the concrete floor.

"What in the world is that?" Rosie asked. She walked around the monstrous machine, running her fingers along the thick metal armor.

"It's called a tank," Bear informed her. "I found it just after the War. No one was around, so I, uh, sort of just borrowed it."

"Borrowed it? From the war? Stole it, you mean." She grinned. "Right?"

"Well, not exactly. After the War, there wasn't anyone around for it to belong to. Or, looking at it another way, since I was one of the very few survivors of what had been the United States Army, it belonged to me as much as it did to anyone. Anyway, I climbed in, turned the switch, and it started right up. So I thought, well, since no one else seems to want it, I'll just take it home. I can always give it back if there's an issue."

"And it's sat here for what, thirty-five years?" Rosie asked.

"About that. A couple of times a year, I dust it off and start it up. Check the weapons systems, lubricate the machine guns. You know, all the little maintenance stuff."

"It has *guns*? You're kidding, right?"

"Not kidding, Rosie Girl. Of course it has guns. Wouldn't be much of a war machine without weapons, would it?"

Rosie climbed to the top of the tank and peered down inside, first into the driver's hatch, then the gunner's hatch. "Wow! This is cool! And we're going shopping in *this*? You've gotta be joking!"

"Nah, I never take this baby out. Bradley lives a quiet life right here in the auto shop."

"Bradley?"

"That's her name. She's a Bradley M2A3, but I just call her Bradley. Brad, mostly."

"Brad is a boy's name."

"She hasn't objected, so far."

"But you *could* take her out if you wanted to?"

"I suppose. But I don't."

"What do you even keep her for, then?"

"I don't know. It's something to do, I guess. Besides, you never know. Anyway, you want to go shopping, or what?"

Rosie hopped down and gave the enormous vehicle a last sideways glance. "Sure. Shopping. But *not* in an army tank."

"Not in an army tank," Bear agreed. "In my shopping cart. Come see."

Rosie went around to the far side of the tank and found Bear standing next to an impossibly small red vehicle. He disconnected a fat power cord from the side of the little car, then straightened up. "Hop in. Dogs, too."

Rosie stared. "Your shopping cart is an electric roller skate?"

The Bear and The Rose

— Chapter 11 —

Hunter

"**V**ery hilarious," Bear said. "You going shopping or not?"

"Okay, okay," Rosie said. She opened the passenger door, worked out how to fold the passenger seat forward, then gestured for the dogs to get in. "After you, Molly. You, too, Bruno." The dogs jumped right in—they'd done this before, many times. Rosie unfolded the passenger seat, then squeezed herself in. Meanwhile, Bear was attempting, mostly unsuccessfully, to wedge his bulk into the driver's seat.

"Maybe if you took off your fur coat," Rosie suggested.

"Again, very hilarious. It's just been a while, that's all." But after a moment, the fur coat sailed through the open driver's door onto Rosie's lap.

Shortly thereafter, a somewhat-compressed Bear squeezed himself behind the wheel, which groaned in protest. "You were right about the coat after all," he growled.

"Too much pizza and cheeseburgers last winter, more likely."

"Yeah," Bear agreed. "Pizza." He pushed a button on a hand-held device, and the huge metal roll-up shop door started lifting. It didn't have far to go before Bear could guide the little car outside, where he pushed the button again and watched to make sure the door closed all the way.

They tootled around to a tall, camouflaged gate, which opened at the push of another button. Again, Bear drove through, pushed the button, and watched until the gate was fully closed. The gate was practically invisible from the outside.

Bear buzzed down the ramp to where Rat and his gang were waiting in their van. Rat rolled down his driver's-side window and tried to stifle a laugh, to no avail. He laughed outright, along with Echo and JR. Then Rosie was laughing, too.

"All right, all right," Bear said. "Let's get going. You've all seen a man drive a car before."

"Well, yes," Rat gasped, "but not one as big as you in a car as small as that. It's going to take all four of us, plus the dogs, to pry you back out of there."

Bear scowled. "Follow me. I'm going to turn left at the first intersection, then go straight west. Think you can keep up?"

Rat stifled another outburst. "Just maybe, if you take it reeeal slow."

Everyone roared with laughter. Bear, disgusted, headed out of the old school parking lot and puttered down the avenue. Rat and his crew followed. Rosie could see them laughing in the little side mirror.

"If we should happen to buy something," Rosie asked with a perfectly straight face, "where, exactly, are we going to put it?"

"Oh, for—"

Rosie cracked up.

Bear said, "It reminds me of a joke that was popular when my grandpa was a kid: How many elephants can you fit into a Volkswagen?"

"What's a Volkswagen?"

"A really small car."

"Smaller than this one?"

Bear narrowed his eyes. "No."

"Well, how many?"

"Nine. Three in the front seat, three in the back seat, two in the trunk, and one in the glove compartment."

"Do you think that joke is funny?"

"I used to." Bear sighed. "Not so much, now."

"Why would anyone put elephants in a car?"

"I don't know. It doesn't matter anymore."

"You know what's funnier?"

"What?"

"How many fuzzy bears, skinny girls, and giant dogs can you fit into a roller skate?"

Bear looked miserable and sank down in the driver's seat as far as he could, which wasn't very far. "Keep your eyes open. We're getting close to the mall now."

"We are? Is that it?" She pointed to a cluster of half-ruined buildings in the middle of a big parking lot.

"Almost," Bear said. "It's that tall building over there." He turned into the old parking lot, swerving to avoid the brush and trees that had grown up through the cracks in the asphalt. He pulled up close to a set of double doors guarded by two men with guns. "Okay, this is it. Out you go."

Rat parked his van next to Bear's little car. He and his gang joined Bear and Rosie by the door.

Rosie and the dogs followed Bear as he approached the two guards slowly, hands in plain sight. The taller of the two recognized him. "Hello, Bear!" he said pleasantly. "It's been a while."

"It has at that. How've you been, Hunter? And who's your friend here?"

"Fair-to-middlin'," Hunter said. "This is Stan. He's been with us for about a year."

"These are my friends." Bear indicated Rat, JR, and Echo. "They're with me. Would you mind keeping an eye on their van, along with my car? Molly and Bruno can stay and help you."

"No problem," Hunter said. "Doing some shopping today?"

"The girls, Miss Echo and my new friend, Miss Rose, here, are in need of new clothes. They were both wounded by the Loward's Fury—Rosie, last night, Echo, this morning.

"Loward's Fury? I heard they were moving out our way, but I haven't seen them yet, personally."

"They chased Rosie into my place last night, guns blazing. They shot her in the side."

Rosie obligingly lifted her shirt tail to show Hunter the bandage on her belly.

Hunter gave a low whistle. "That was a close one. A little higher…"

"Yeah," Bear said. "Echo's was a leg wound, just a graze, but her pants were ruined. Anyway, Rosie's under my protection now, same as Rat and his gang. Pass the word, if you don't mind."

"Sure thing, Bear," Hunter said agreeably. "I'm sure it won't be a problem. Almost everyone around here is in your debt one way or another." He grinned. "And that includes me. I haven't forgotten the food you gave me and Angela last winter. We wouldn't have made it without you."

"It was my pleasure. What do you know about a kid named Jimmy? Was working with Rat's gang until this morning. He came in with them when we patched up Echo."

Hunter spat on the sidewalk. "I hope you sent him packing. He's bad news, if you ask me."

"In fact, I *did* send him packing. He was rude and disrespectful, and much too interested in Rosie and Echo. I made it pretty clear that it was in his best interests that I never see him again. I hope he has sense enough to believe that."

"Did you show him your ball field?" Hunter grinned.

"Nah, but I did mention it. I think he got the idea."

"Hope so," Hunter said dubiously, "but I wouldn't count on it."

"What do you recommend for outfitting this gang?"

Hunter thought it over. "Couple of new guys on the second floor, just up the first stairway on the right. Brought a lot of stuff in over the last week or two. Maybe they've got something your kids can use. They have men's clothes, too, in case you're feeling generous."

Bear laughed out loud. "Me? Generous? Please, Hunter, keep it low—you want to spoil my reputation?"

"I'd never think of it, Bear. Happy shopping!"

The Bear and The Rose

92

— Chapter 12 —

The Mall

Rosie stopped just inside the door. Her feet didn't want to move. The mall was full of movement and sound. Piles and piles of salvaged goods were heaped everywhere. Dozens of people were running to and fro, from one pile to another, shouting to each other. Many of them carried stacks of goods. Some even had little carts piled high with things Rosie couldn't identify.

Bear let her look for a while, then asked, "Rosie? You coming or not?"

"I… I've… never seen this many people in my entire life. There must be… fifty? A hundred?"

"A lot more than that, on a busy day," Bear said.

JR added in his quiet voice, "On a busy day, there might be as many as two thousand."

"I didn't know there were that many people left in the world!" Rosie said.

"There are, Rosie," Echo said, "but a good many of them aren't friendly, and you need to be careful, okay?"

Rat said, "Don't take this wrong, Rosie, but you're a pretty girl. And there are plenty of people who would steal you if they had a chance."

"Steal me?" She looked at Bear. "You mean for… having—?"

"And worse," Bear said, his face settling into a grim line. "Some of these folks are okay, but far too many of them are out for themselves and anything they can get. Best you stick close to me and the gang, okay? Goes for you, too, Echo, but I'm sure you know that already."

"Yes, Bear," Echo said. She turned to Rosie. "I've been here lots of times, because of scavenging, you know. Sometimes we sell stuff here. But I would never, ever, come here without Rat and JR. And they are always armed." She pulled a vicious-looking switchblade a few inches out of her front pants pocket, just far enough for Rosie to see it, then shoved it back down. "Me, too."

Rosie was taken aback. After a moment to recover, she asked Bear, "Should I be armed, too? I wouldn't know what to do with a knife like that."

"No, you wouldn't," Bear said. "Which is exactly why you shouldn't have one. Later on, if you want, I'll give you a little training, and you can decide what you want to do."

Rosie nodded, then asked Echo, "Did you get training? From Mr. The Bear?"

Echo nodded. "We all did, all three of us. Bare-knuckle, knives, and guns, too."

Rat patted his jacket pocket, but his face didn't change.

"Where… uh…" Rosie closed her mouth.

Bear said, "We can talk about training later. You've got plenty on your plate right now. Let's go up the stairs, see if we can find the clothes vendor that Hunter mentioned."

"These are funny stairs," Rosie said. "They're metal. I've never seen stairs like this before."

"It's called an escalator," Bear said, "which is just a fancy word for stairs. Before the War, when there was plenty of electricity, these stairs moved."

Rosie looked doubtful. "I wish I could have seen that."

"I saw it," Bear said. "Before the War. When the War started, you know, I was just a little older than you. So I remember the old world and how things were. And yes, the escalator was fun to ride. When I was just a little kid, my cousin and I would go around and around, for hours, sometimes, until the mall security came and chased us away." He laughed. "We didn't care, though—we'd just go to the escalators at the other end of the mall."

The new clothing vendors Hunter had mentioned occupied a kind of storefront that consisted of a row of folding tables lined up in front of a sort of metal gate. Rosie looked it over and decided that when the store closed, the vendors could drag the tables inside, then lower the gate for a measure of protection against theft. She wondered how in the world anyone could get into the mall to steal something and hope to get out again without getting caught by the guards.

There were a few really nice-looking garments on the tables, but, behind the gate, the place was positively stuffed with heaps and piles of clothing, in all colors and sizes. Behind the tables, two men and a woman waited to assist shoppers.

Rosie looked the woman over. She was maybe about Rosie's mother's age, around forty, Rosie guessed. But unlike her mother, this woman seemed bright and alert. Her brunette hair was done up in an attractive style, and she was even wearing earrings and a necklace. And shiny colored bracelets on both wrists. Her jeans were tight, showing her figure, and her shirt was bright red. Rosie's mother would have been shocked beyond belief. The Loward's Own didn't hold with vanity, especially in females.

The men looked pretty sharp, too. Their hair was trimmed neatly and combed. One of them had a tiny clock he wore on a bracelet on his left wrist. Both of them were dressed in what appeared to be brand-new jeans, with turned-up cuffs. Their shoes were new and matched their wide brown belts, which were fastened with big shiny buckles. One of the buckles featured a picture of a cow. The other had some sort of large boxy vehicle. They wore matching plaid flannel shirts and straw cowboy hats.

The younger of the two doffed his hat at Rosie, and said, "Welcome, little lady! How can we be of service to you today?"

A wave of shyness flooded unbidden over Rosie. She blushed, stared at the floor, and backed away from the man.

"No worries, little lady. I'll be here when you're ready." He turned to Bear. "How about you, sir? May I be of some small service?"

"Sure thing, pardner," Bear said in an accent strange to Rosie. "I'm looking to fix up my friends here with some new duds. They're all gonna need shirts and pants and socks and whatnot. And the little lady here"—he indicated Rosie, who had migrated to Bear's side—"is going to need…" Bear ran his hand over his belly, describing an imaginary baby bump.

The woman smiled kindly at Rosie. "Come here, child. Let me look at you."

Rosie was apparently rooted to her spot next to Bear, who gave her a not-so-gentle shove toward the woman.

The vendor lady smiled warmly, extending her arms in welcome. "Oh, look at you! Don't you look pretty!" She nodded toward Rosie's belly. "May I?"

Rosie glanced at Bear, who nodded. "Okay," Rosie said, but she sounded doubtful.

"I'm Kathy," the woman announced. She ran her hand gently over Rosie's incipient belly bump, then smiled. "About three months along?"

"About," Rosie managed to croak out.

"Well, you are surely going to need some baby-mama clothes real soon, then. You wait right here, and I'll see what I can find. I'm sure there must be plenty—it's been a very long time since anyone wanted baby-mama clothes." A tear escaped and ran down her cheek. "My husband and I wanted a baby, you know. We tried so hard. But I just couldn't seem to conceive." She brushed away the tear. "Now my husband's dead and I'm too old to have a baby. It's not my fault, you know. Lots of women can't have babies now. I heard once that there was something in the bombs that did something bad to women's baby-making equipment." She pointed at her own abdomen. "You know, here, inside." She took a long, deep breath, wiped her eyes, and said brightly, "Well, honey, you surely are the lucky one, to have a baby of your own. Let's get you fixed up. What do you say, hon?" She looked Rosie up and down, checking for size, then turned and disappeared among the stacks of clothing inside the store.

As she waited, Rosie watched the two fancy men measure Rat and JR. Echo presented herself for measurement, too, but the men said it would be better for Echo to wait until Kathy came back. That seemed to meet with Bear's approval. After Rat and JR were measured, one of the men vanished into the dim interior. The other introduced himself to Bear and the boys.

"My name, by the way, is Dale. The other fellow is Evan, my brother. Our sister is Kathy. We're new in this here mall, which is why you probably haven't met us yet. May I ask, sir, if you are a regular patron of this mall?"

"I've been known to come around from time to time," Bear said. "People call me Bear. Pleased to meet you both." Bear stuck out a giant paw and solemnly shook hands with each of the brothers. "Hunter, the guard at the south gate, is a friend of mine. He suggested we give you a try."

"Why, that's mighty kind of him," Dale said. "I'll remember to thank him when next I see him. If you don't mind me asking, Mr. Bear—"

"Just 'Bear'."

"Of course, Bear. Do you have a particular budget in mind, and how might you be paying?"

Bear narrowed his eyes, then decided it was a fair question, under the circumstances. He checked up and down the length of the mezzanine floor. Most of the vendor spaces were vacant. As far as Bear could see, he was the only customer in sight. He stuck his paw into his fur coat's massive side pocket, then withdrew it, his fist clenched. He beckoned Dale to lean in closer, opened his fingers for a heartbeat, revealing a small glass vial, then closed it.

Dale goggled. "Is that—"

"Penicillin," Bear whispered.

"Pure?"

Bear narrowed his eyes.

"Of course it's pure," Dale babbled. "I meant no offense, of course. It's just that I've never seen—" He caught his breath. "May I assume, then, that your budget is virtually unlimited today?"

Bear nodded slowly. "I'd like the kids to have something nice for a change. Do you think we can manage that, for this?" He nodded toward his closed hand.

"Oh, yes, I'm sure we can. No problem, sir, no problem at all."

"And I'm sure I don't have to mention that you don't have a clue where this came from, right?"

"Absolutely right, sir, of course. I know nothing about it. Anonymous stranger, and all that."

"Good."

"And how about you, sir? Would you like to look at something for yourself?"

"I'm fine."

"As you say, Bear."

Evan returned, bearing stacks of boys' jeans, shirts, boots, socks, hats, underwear, and even a couple of fleece-lined winter coats. "Let's try these on, boys," Evan said. "Once we know what fits, we can supply everything you need. He distributed various garments to Rat and JR who, without hesitation, began peeling off their old clothes.

A moment later, Kathy brought a stack of girls' clothes. She noted the boys' activity, then called Rosie and Echo. "Come with me, girls. We have something called 'changing booths' just inside. I'm sure you'll prefer that to what the boys are doing. *Boys!* Hmph!"

The girls laughed and followed Kathy inside.

A half-hour later, the boys and girls were all decked out in new or nearly-new jeans, shirts, and winter clothes. Everyone had a well-fitting pair of boots and a warm hat, too. They were all smiles and laughter and chattering animatedly.

Dale timidly approached Bear. "Mr.—uh, Bear, I'm very sorry, but all those clothes don't come close to the value of—"

"Don't worry about it," Bear said. "You can keep it on account. If any one of these kids comes to you for anything, you can charge it against whatever you think you owe me. I'll trust you to keep track. How's that sound? Also, my friend Hunter's wife could use some new clothes. Maybe you can find something for her."

Dale, relieved, said. "Oh, thank you, Bear. I was nearly beside myself trying to figure out what to do."

"One more thing," Bear said. "If you should run across someone who is in desperate need of clothes, you can fix them up, too, and charge it to me. If you run over, I'll square up with you next time I'm at the mall. Okay?"

"Certainly, Bear. It will be my pleasure."

"Good," Bear said. "You kids ready? Let's go. It's nearly suppertime."

Down the escalator they went, in high spirits, the boys trying to slide down the old rubber railings. There was quite a crowd of shoppers downstairs now. "Stay close," Bear told the kids, as he plowed a channel through the crowd.

When they got outside, Bear nodded to Hunter. "Excellent suggestion, the new guys upstairs. They seem like a nice little family."

"That was my impression," Hunter said. "I'm glad it worked out."

"Angela likely needs some new clothes—you can get them upstairs. Just tell them it's on my account. I overpaid a little—they didn't have any change, you know."

Hunter laughed. "Naturally. Well, thank you, Bear. I don't know how you do it, but you're a great help to me and my family, and I'm sure to many others, as well. If you ever need anything at all, just say a word."

"I'll do that," Bear said. They clasped hands.

Bruno whined and pawed at the glass door.

"Bear!" Rosie tugged at his coat sleeve. "Echo and the boys—they didn't come out of the mall!"

— Chapter 13 —

Borrowed from the War

"They were right behind me," Bear said. "Didn't you see them?"

"They were with us at the bottom of the metal stairs," Rosie said. "After that, I'm not sure. Do you suppose they just got sidetracked in the crowd?"

"Wait here with Hunter," Bear commanded. "I'm going back in."

Rosie pressed her nose to the glass panes next to the doors and watched Bear as he disappeared into the crowd. He was much taller than most of the shoppers, so she monitored his progress until he disappeared up the metal stairs, far inside the mall.

Bear scanned the mezzanine floor, but there was no one in sight. He headed to the clothing booth, where he found Evan and Kathy treating a gunshot wound in Dale's upper right arm.

"What happened?" Bear demanded.

Tears ran down Dale's face. "I'm sorry, Bear. I tried to stop him. I grabbed hold of him, but I let go when he shot me. It wasn't my fault, I swear."

"Okay, calm down. I'm not mad at you. I just want to find my kids, Echo and the two boys, and the sooner the better."

"He didn't have kids with him."

"Tell me what happened, from the beginning. Think you can do that? Take a deep breath and slow down."

Kathy put the finishing touches on a makeshift bandage she'd fashioned from a big red bandanna.

Dale began, "A few moments after you all left, as soon as you were out of sight down the stairs, this kid comes up and points a pistol at me. He says to give him the penicillin, or he'll kill us all. So I handed it over. He put it in his vest pocket, then said, 'Oh, and tell the Bear Man that if he ever wants to see the little girly-girl and her boyfriends again, he should go back to his playground and wait for a message.' Then he turned to leave. That's when I grabbed his shoulder, and he shot me, just like that! And then he ran off."

"Which way?"

"The other way, north." He pointed up the long mezzanine.

"He's long gone by now," Bear said. "I don't have another penicillin for you, I'm sorry."

"It's hardly your fault, Mr. Bear." Dale got shakily to his feet. "How can we help? We'll do anything we can."

"We sure will, Bear," Kathy said. "I liked that little filly."

"I'll let you know," Bear said. "I appreciate the offer."

"Least we could do," Evan said. "If we see that guy again, what should we do?"

"You won't see him again," Bear said. "But just in case, if he does show up here, tell Hunter at the south gate. He'll know what to do. Was there anything about the guy that you'd even recognize again? How was he dressed?"

Kathy said, "Raggedy old jeans, jean jacket, gray t-shirt with a pocket, flat black hat, grubby old black boots, needed a shine."

"So," Bear said, "he looked like nearly everyone else here."

"Sorry, Bear," Evan said, "but that's about the size of it."

"What will you do?" Dale asked.

"No much *to* do, really. I'm going to go home and wait for instructions. After that, we'll have to see. You folks take care. Don't take any chances."

"We won't," Kathy said. "One thing, though—will you let us know what happens?"

"I'll be back," Bear said, "one way or the other." Back at the south gate, Rosie deluged Bear with a thousand questions, none of which he could answer. "I'll just have to follow the instructions, for now. That's all there is." And to Hunter he said, "Right now it's sit-and-wait time. I'll let you know what I find out, if I can."

"I'll tell the rest of the guards," Hunter said. "You'll have all the help you need."

"While you're at it," Bear said, "spread the news of a fat reward for any help in getting the kids back."

"Will do, Bear. I hope you find them."

"I'll find them." He turned to Rosie. "Let's go home. You're going to have to drive the shopping cart. I'll drive Rat's van."

"What? Me, drive?"

"Sure, why not? It's not rocket science. Right-side foot pedal makes it go forward. Left-side pedal makes it stop. Steering wheel makes it turn. Just be in control, make it do what you want it to do. Anyway, you'll be following me, and I'll take it slow. Molly! Bruno! Load up!"

Rosie, looking doubtful but determined, followed the dogs into the little electric car and situated herself behind the wheel. She tried the Go pedal, then, a little abruptly, the Stop pedal. "Okay, Mr. The Bear. I've got it."

"Good. Follow me." He climbed into Rat's van and slowly left the mall parking lot, Rosie close behind.

Back at Bear's compound, Bear parked the van in front of the main entrance, and Rosie rolled the little shopping cart to a stop right behind him. He and Rosie made a beeline for the administration offices.

"Right, then," Bear said. "Let's check our weapons while we wait." In the principal's office, he unlocked a concealed door behind a painting, revealing a small arsenal cabinet containing racks of all sorts of weapons: automatic rifles, pistols, knives, bayonets, and even a few swords.

He chose an assault rifle and a pair of Mossberg pistol-grip combat shotguns. He gave Rosie a smaller but vicious-looking submachine gun.

"Borrow these from the War, too?" Rosie asked.

"Yeah," Bear said. "Turns out the original owners didn't have any further use for them. I don't really, either. I brought them here and cleaned them up, just in case. No point in letting them rust away. I haven't used them for a very long time, but I keep them cleaned and oiled. Like I said, you never know."

"Right," Rosie said.

"We might not use them at all," Bear said. "We'll see what the messenger has to say. Meanwhile, let's get you checked out on this hardware, then get ourselves some chow."

"Sounds good to me," Rosie said. "What's for supper?"

"How about some sandwiches? I made some yesterday before Echo arrived."

"Sounds fine to me."

"I have to stay here and watch for the messenger," Bear said. "Up in the watchtower. Can you run to the kitchen and grab the bag of sandwiches? Maybe some apples, too. And a jug of water. Take the dogs with you."

Rosie called the dogs and sprinted for the cafeteria. When she got back, Bear was still in the watchtower, so Rosie carried the food up the stairs. After they ate, they took half-hour turns peering through the gun ports. It was a long, tedious vigil. Bear was anxious about his friends, and his anxiety rubbed off on Rosie.

Just as it was growing dark, the dogs whined and their ears pricked. Bear scanned the street, but saw nothing. He shook Rosie gently. "Rosie, wake up. The dogs just went on alert. Look sharp, now!"

"Okay, Bear. I'm watching." She rubbed the sleep out of her eyes and looked out into the dusk. "Nothing coming up the road in either direction." She kept looking, then, "Hold on, I see some movement to the south. Nothing definite yet."

"Keep watching."

"I'm watching," Rosie said. "A single light just came on. Might be a motorcycle… definitely a motorcycle, and moving fast."

Bear selected one of the assault rifles. "Lock the door after me." Bear dashed downstairs and outside to the main entrance. He unlocked the chain but held the door closed. A few seconds later, the motorcycle roared into the school parking lot without slowing down. Bear worked the bolt on his rifle, set it to burst fire, then opened the door a crack. He took careful aim and fired just as the rider lobbed a dark object over the front wall.

All three bullets penetrated the gas tank on the motorcycle. The rider braked so hard that he flew over the handlebars onto the asphalt. The wrecked motorcycle exploded into flames behind him.

Bear ran to the fallen rider, grabbed the shoulder of his leather jacket, and dragged him inside the compound. Rosie came out to the courtyard and stood guard over the rider while Bear secured the front entrance. The rider made a move to get up, but Rosie shook her head and pressed the muzzle of her SMG against the rider's forehead.

Bear retrieved the dark object the rider had thrown. It was a note tied around a rock. "How… original," Bear said. He read the note. "If you want your girly-girl and her boyfriends back alive, meet us at the entrance to Teakettle's corral at midnight. Bring five vials of penicillin, or the girl gets it." Bear laughed. "These guys have been watching too many old-time vids." He imitated an ancient gangster's voice: "Meet me at midnight and have da goods witcha, or da bunny gets it, see?"

"I don't get it," Rosie said. "What bunny? Do you mean Echo? Is Echo the bunny?"

"Never mind," Bear said. "It's just how the movies—the vids—were when I was a little kid. And they were old, then."

Bear hauled the battered rider to his feet. "Tell your master that we'll be there at midnight." He dragged the rider to the front entrance and shoved him outside. "Now, git! If I see you again, I'll kill you."

Back inside the principal's office, Bear plopped his bulk down into one of the padded chairs and took another sandwich. "Tank up," he told Rosie. "There won't be anything else tonight."

"How can you be sure?"

"Wouldn't make sense," Bear said. "The next move is at the Teakettle's corral."

"I'll bet a lot could go wrong there," Rosie mumbled around a mouthful of apple.

"Yes, it could," Bear said. "We'll have to plan carefully. Fortunately, we have a few hours before we have to be there."

Bear finished his sandwich and went to the arsenal cabinet. He put on a military web belt and gave one to Rosie. "Here, put this on."

She took a moment to figure out the clasp, then adjusted it to fit her slim hips. "What are all these little pouches for?"

"Glad you asked," Bear said, and handed her several boxes of ammunition and magazines. "Here—let's trade your SMG for this assault rifle. You might need a little extra firepower tonight. These little metal things are called clips. You fill them with ammunition, like this." He demonstrated. "Then the clips fit into the pouches on your belt."

Rosie followed Bear's example until all her clips were full. Then Bear went back to the cabinet and fetched combat knives, flashlights, water bottles, and medical kits.

"Looks like we're going to start another war, ourselves," Rosie observed.

"Let's hope not," Bear said. "I've had enough war for a lifetime. What we want from tonight is a clean, safe exchange. They get the penicillin, we get Echo and the boys. No threats, no insults, no bandying of words of any kind. We're going to be all business and totally pro. Right?"

Rosie nodded, looking sober and serious.

"But if we have to fight," Bear continued, "if we absolutely have to fight, I want a quick, decisive win. Aim for the center of their bodies and keep firing until they're dead." He searched Rosie's face. "Do you think you can fire on another human being?"

Rosie nodded slowly. "I think so. If I have to."

"Right," Bear said. "Don't shoot unless absolutely necessary, but if you have to shoot, shoot to kill. But, that having been said, I'm not expecting trouble. These jerks probably overheard our exchange with the vendors at the mall and decided to go into the penicillin business. Silly of them—they might have just talked to me."

"Would you really have given them some?" Rosie asked.

"No, of course not. I would have explained to them that I only had the one bottle, didn't know how to get more, then directed them to the guy I wholesale them to. I have a guy in the capital, close to Johnson himself, who takes charge of what I produce. He makes sure that anyone who needs it can get it, even if they can't afford it. There's a little slush room built into the price."

"Do you even *have* five vials of penicillin? Where do you get them, anyway?" Rosie caught herself. "Sorry, pretend I didn't ask that. None of my business."

"It's a family secret," Bear said, "but you're family now. I make it in the school's old biology lab. Why are you crying?"

"I'm not crying," Rosie insisted. She wiped her eyes on her sleeve. "I just like being your family, that's all."

"Well," Bear assured her, "you *are* family. Since the War, and even before then, families all over the world have gotten mixed up and scrambled. It's up to each one of us to choose the best family we can for ourselves."

Rosie turned away so Bear couldn't see her leaking again. "So, how do you make penicillin, anyway?"

Bear laughed. "It's not hard if you know how. Like just about everything else. It's made from mold."

Rosie looked skeptical. "Mold?"

"Well, not just any kind of mold, and there are things you have to do to process it to make it safe for humans and animals. But, yes, it's made from a kind of mold commonly found on stale bread or old fruit. It's science, but not all that complicated. If you know how."

"But, Mr. The Bear," Rosie said, "you could be rich."

"I am rich," Bear said. "Don't you think so?"

Rosie thought it over. "I guess you are. I never thought of you as being rich, though. But you have everything you need and extra to help others with. I suppose that's rich."

"It's as rich as I ever wanted to be," Bear said. "But you forgot one thing."

"What's that?"

"I'm rich in friends, too," Bear said. "Friends like you. And like Rat and his gang."

"And Hunter and his wife," Rosie said. "And I bet there are many more like them, aren't there? People you've helped over the years, who would do anything for you?"

"I like to think so," Bear said, "but I hope I never have to call on them for anything. Gather your gear, now. It's about time we headed out."

Bear closed up the armory, locked it securely, slid the panels back in place, then rearranged the furniture so that a casual observer would never suspect the armory was there.

— Chapter 14 —

GUNFIGHT AT THE TEAKETTLE CORRAL

ROSIE ASKED, "So, Mr, The Bear, how are we going to get to this place? Is it far?"

"It's about two miles," Bear said. "And it's right off a main avenue. There's enough debris in the road that it might be faster to walk. We could walk it in forty minutes or so, but then we'd have to carry all this gear. Also, if we needed a hasty retreat, we'd be in trouble. What do you think?"

"I think we should take the Bradley," Rosie said. "Just to encourage them to keep their word."

"It would, at that," Bear said. "But it would also ruin the surprise."

"What surprise? I like surprises!"

"The surprise is that I have a working Bradley. Someday I might really need it for something dire. But if people found out I have one in the meantime, they'd be over here all the time trying to steal it. Not that they could, or that I'd permit it, but it would keep me busy protecting it all the time. And once that secret is out, it's out forever. There'd be no going back."

"How will you know when it's the right time to use it?"

"I'll know," Bear said. "We all will. Instead, we'll take the shopping cart to about a hundred feet from the meeting spot, then walk the rest of the way as quietly as we can."

They gathered their gear and carried it out to the shopping cart, still parked in front. Bear checked the shopping cart's power level. It was still nearly at full charge.

When they had finished loading the shopping cart, Bear said, "I'm going to put Molly and Bruno in my room until we get back. Wait for me—it won't take long."

He led the dogs down the hallway, put them in his private room, and returned.

"Don't they mind getting left behind?"

"A bit," Bear explained, "but I fed them and gave them some treats. I do it from time to time. They've become accustomed to it. Don't worry, they'll be fine. Okay, then, ready to go? It's getting dark."

Bear threaded his way among the ruins of the motorcycle, and eased the little vehicle onto the roadway, heading south this time, in the opposite direction from the mall.

They drove south for a couple of long blocks, then east for a couple more, until they approached an odd five-way intersection. There was a ruined school on one corner and an old church on another. It was hard to say what denomination the church originally served, but now the low, wooden sign on the corner boasted a hand-drawn, spray-painted scrawl, 'Church of the Loward.' It was a moderately sized compound, with the actual church building on the corner. Behind it stretched a couple of rows of classrooms or dormitories or barracks or something arranged around an asphalted courtyard.

Bear and Rosie watched the church for ten minutes or so from a safe distance, but saw neither a bit of light nor a flicker of movement.

"Do you think there's anyone using that place?" Rosie asked.

"Hard to say," Bear said. "It looks quiet, but, well, you never know. Let's park here, just to be on the safe side." He turned the shopping cart around and parked it on a little gravel strip by the edge of the road. They took their gear and crept through the underbrush at the edge of the road until they came to a small clearing in front of a wooden barricade that had once sported a ROAD CLOSED sign. Behind the barricade, a narrow old street penetrated the dense foliage of the neighborhood.

Bear pointed at an area that had once been fenced for horses: wooden posts and broad cross-boards painted white long ago. A few posts remained upright, the white paint peeling in long strips. "That's Teakettle's corral. I used to play there when I was a kid, before the War."

"Why is it called that?" Rosie wanted to know. "Did they sell tea or something?"

"No, no," Bear said. "The name of the people who lived there was Teakettle, or something like that. Everyone called them the Teakettle girls. I knew them since the third grade. Connie was my age, and her sister, Karen, was a year older."

"Were you in love with one of them?" Rosie asked.

"Not exactly. My best friend, Topher, and I used to ride our bicycles over here and throw horse droppings at them."

"Ewww!" Rosie cried. "That's… disgusting!"

"Oh, I don't know," Bear said. "Horse poop is basically just grass and water. We didn't care. And Connie and Karen threw plenty at us, too. They kept horses in the corral, two or three of them, so there was always plenty of ammunition."

"Boys are horrible!" Rosie said.

"At ten years old, we thought girls were icky," Bear said. "We changed our minds a few years later, though. Enough talk for now."

Slowly and quietly, they walked fifty feet along the tree line of the old, winding street, until they could just barely make out a handful of silhouettes against the ambient light.

"Wait here," Bear said. "Ready your assault rifle, take aim, but don't fire unless I signal."

"Right," Rosie whispered. "What's the signal?"

"I'll yell my head off, okay?"

Rosie knelt in the dewy grass by the crumbling edge of the old asphalt road. She assumed a half-sitting position as Bear had shown her, worked the bolt on her weapon, and found a target in her sights.

Bear advanced slowly, holding his empty hands out by his sides. There was no sign of the two combat shotguns slung inside his great fur coat. When he reached the little clearing alongside the old corral, a voice called out, "Hold it right there." Bear stopped, but said nothing.

"Do you have the penicillin?" The voice was familiar.

"Yes. Is that you, Jimmy? I recognize your voice."

"Never mind who I am," Jimmy said. "Let's see the penicillin."

"It's in my coat pocket," Bear said. "Can I reach for it without getting shot?"

"Go ahead," Jimmy said.

Slowly, slowly, Bear reached into his left-hand coat pocket and extracted five penicillin vials, then carefully held them up for inspection.

"Toss them over."

"Am I that stupid? Show me my kids."

Several youths dragged Echo and the boys forward.

"Here they are," Jimmy said. "Now toss the penicillin over."

Bear tossed the little packet of five vials about halfway toward Jimmy. "There it is. Tell your boys to bring the kids over. They can leave the kids and pick up the packet."

Jimmy had to think this over. "Okay. Go ahead, guys. Easy does it. Just drop off the kids and pick up the drugs."

"Don't fight them, Rat," Bear called out. "Just go along with them."

"Shut up, Bear," Jimmy roared. "Try anything, and my guys will shoot you down, and the kids along with you."

"And that would be the last thing they ever did," Bear said quietly. "And you'll be the first to go, Jimmy. So keep that in mind and let's just make the deal."

"Fine, whatever, just shut up, okay?" Jimmy was almost screaming.

"Okay, okay," Bear said. "Easy, now."

The boys reached the spot where the little packet lay on the ground. They gave Echo and the boys one last shove, propelling them toward Bear, then bent to retrieve the penicillin.

Echo ran into Bear's outstretched arms. "Oh, Bear, I'm so sorry."

"Quiet now," Bear whispered. "Everything's okay. Let's just back away. Get behind me and stay there. I have two shotguns under my coat. Stay out of my line of fire. Rosie's waiting for you in the trees. Understand?"

She nodded, then she and the boys slipped behind Bear, and fast-walked toward the trees, crouching instinctively.

Bear took a few tentative steps backward. It looked good, everybody was staying cool.

Jimmy's gang leader held the packet of Penicillin high above his head. "I got it, Jimmy. It looks like the real stuff."

And the gang leader's head disappeared in a cloud of pink mist, followed by the sound of a shot.

"Run, kids!" Bear yelled. The two combat shotguns appeared magically in his hands. Before he could aim, however, there were more shots, and Jimmy was down, along with the rest of his crew.

Bear turned and ran back to Rosie's position. "Why did you shoot them? It was going just fine."

"I didn't," Rosie said. "I never fired at all."

"Who did, then?" Bear asked.

"I don't know," Rosie said. "I was watching you."

"The shots came from the other side of the corral, through the trees across the road," Rat reported.

"I was scanning the trees," JR said. "I didn't see anything."

"Let's retreat to the shopping cart," Bear said. "Maybe we can still get out of here."

The five of them moved slowly toward the old wooden barricade but stopped when a lone figure stepped into the clearing by the corral, a long sniper rifle cradled in his arms. He strolled to the gang leader's body and nudged it with his toe. "Dead," he called out, then rolled the body over, revealing the packet of vials. He picked them up and looked them over. "None broken," he said.

As he inspected the other bodies, Rosie kept him in her telescopic sights. "He's wearing a uniform," she said in a monotone. "Blue, with silver angels. It's the Loward's Fury. We have to get out of here *now*!"

"Let's *move*!" Bear commanded. "Into the shopping cart, quick as you can." They dashed to the gravel strip where the shopping cart was parked.

Two dozen young men and women stepped out of the trees behind the shopping cart and pointed various firearms toward Bear and the four kids. All were wearing the same blue uniform with various rank insignia, and all had the silver angels. One young man, with more insignia than the others, stepped forward. "You must be the one called Bear. I can see why. Would you be so kind as to hand over those shotguns you carry under your fur coat, along with any other weapons you might have?" When Bear hesitated the young man said, "We can try to take them from you if you prefer, but I'm afraid some of your people might get hurt. My men have orders to shoot the girls first, then the boys. They're saving you for last. It's up to you—care to give it a try?"

Bear sagged. He and Rosie might get a few of them, but there were just too many. The kids would die for sure, as would he. Sometimes you just run out of choices. "We'll cooperate." Bear said, his voice tight.

"But—" Rosie began.

"Forget it, Rosie. We're outnumbered. If we try anything, we'll all die, starting with you and Echo. Is that what you'd choose?"

"Yes! I mean No! I mean—"

"Just hand them your weapons, and let's see where this goes, okay?"

Reluctantly, Rosie complied.

"Very wise," the young officer said. "We are the Loward's Fury, but we're a special little group. Unlike most of the Loward's Fury, we answer directly to His Holiness, the Most High Quaestor, The Iron Sceptre himself." He puffed out his chest a little.

Bear frowned a little and repeated, "His Holiness, the Most High Quaester, The Iron Sceptre. Say, when you meet with him, do you have to say all those things every time you address him?"

The young officer replied, rather sheepishly, "Well, I've never actually met him, myself. My superior officer has, though."

"Oh, really?" Bear said. "What does your superior officer call him, then?"

"Um." The young officer was strangely reluctant to answer. "Uh, well, my superior just calls him 'Bob.'"

Rat cracked up, then the girls and JR, then some of the Loward's Fury. Even Bear smiled a little.

"Stop it!" the young officer raged. "Enough of this foolishness!" His face flamed red. "Sergeant, have you collected all their weapons?"

The sergeant put on his best military face. "Yes, sir."

"Searched the"—he sneered—"car? If you can call it that."

"I call it the Roller Skate," Rosie offered, which prompted another round of giggles from the Loward's Fury.

"SHUT *UP!*" the officer roared. "We march. Troops, box formation to the outpost."

The troops formed a box around Bear and the kids, and, in this fashion, they marched to the outpost. Which turned out to be the church across the street.

— Chapter 15 —

The Loward's Fury

WITH GREAT POMP and ceremony, the young officer marched his captives across the street to the church complex. They passed the actual church building, and were admitted into a utility building divided into individual offices. With no spoken command, the four kids were separated and put in the charge of a pair of soldiers, then diverted into an adjoining corridor.

Bear opened his mouth to protest, but a jab in the back with the end of a bayonet changed his mind. "Don't worry about them," the young officer said. "You're about to have troubles enough of your own."

"If you so much as touch them—"

"You'll what? You're in no position to do much of anything, are you?"

Bear growled but said nothing.

At a wooden door at the end of the hallway, the young officer knocked twice.

"Enter."

The guards shoved Bear roughly through the door, into an elaborately appointed office. A middle-aged man wearing a Loward's Fury uniform with US Army major's insignia said, "There's no need to be rough with a prisoner who is cooperating, Captain Hensley. I'm sure Mr.… Bear, is it?" He consulted a list of names on the desk before him. "Yes, Mr. Bear. I'm sure Mr. Bear will behave himself. Uncuff him, please, then you are dismissed."

Captain Hensley directed the two guards to remove Bear's chains, then the three soldiers left the room without a word. *Waiting in the corridor, no doubt,* thought Bear, rubbing his wrists. "There was no need for all the fuss, Major…?"

"Diamond, Major Arnold P. Diamond. Perhaps there wasn't, and if so, I apologize. We need to have a chat with you."

"You might have simply asked," Bear said mildly. "I'm not really disagreeable when you get to know me."

Major Diamond smiled grimly. "I suppose we'll see about that. Have a seat, if you please, Mr. Bear."

Bear wedged his bulk into one of the two 'visitor chairs' in front of the major's desk. "Before we go on, Major, I'd like to know what you plan to do with my kids."

"Oh, you don't need to be concerned about them," Major Diamond replied. "They'll be fine, just fine—as long as you remain cooperative, that is."

Bear frowned. "Is that a threat, Major? I don't respond well to threats, especially against my family."

"No, no, not at all, definitely not a threat. Just a fact. The kids are being fed as we speak. Their continued good treatment is entirely in your hands, Mr. Bear."

"Uh-huh," Bear said skeptically. "What is it you want of me, Major?"

"All in good time. May I offer you some refreshment, perhaps?"

"Let's just get on with it."

"As you wish. Let me begin by introducing myself. I am Major Arnold P. Diamond of the Eighth troop of The Loward's Fury. As I'm sure you know, we are the military arm of The Loward's

Own. Among other things, we encourage compliance with the Loward's righteous standards, and bring new territories into the Loward's fold."

"'Encourage.' Right," Bear said.

"Precisely," Major Diamond agreed. "At this moment in time, we are in the process of annexing the Ard Forest district. We have selected this old church to be our temporary district headquarters until we can acquire a larger complex—an old high school, perhaps."

"I haven't noticed you in the neighborhood until now," Bear said. "Then again, I don't get out much."

"Yes," the Major replied, "we've been keeping an eye on you and we're aware of your activities. We were following you earlier today on your little excursion to the mall. We saw you slip the clothing vendors a vial of penicillin. Or, to be accurate, what we assumed was either penicillin or something equally valuable. Our observer tracked you back to your high school fortress and subsequently intercepted Jimmy's messenger after he delivered his note."

"I didn't see anyone following us," Bear said. "And I was watching."

"Yes, she's good, isn't she? Clever girl. Perhaps you'll meet her one day."

"So all you had to do was wait for us to meet with Jimmy's gang, then muscle in."

"Exactly!" said the Major. "It worked out quite well, I must say."

"For you, maybe. Not so much for Jimmy."

"Despicable creature," the Major declared. "Good riddance to him and his gutter snipes. The world is improved by their absence."

"A Christian point of view, certainly," Bear offered, deadpan.

The Major searched Bear's face, found nothing suspicious, and continued. "And we ended up with the medicine."

"My medicine," Bear said.

"Not anymore," the Major declared. "It has been legally and righteously appropriated for use by the Loward's Own. Don't worry, I assure you it will be used to help many sick ones."

"You might have just asked," Bear said again. "I'm not that hard to get along with."

A uniformed messenger knocked, then entered. He approached Major Diamond, whispered in his ear, and retreated.

Major Diamond smiled. "Our lab has finished their analysis. It seems your vials contained pure, or nearly pure, penicillin. We need to know how and where you obtain it, if you please."

"Or if I don't please, I suppose." Bear sighed. "Fine. I make it myself in the high school's biology classroom. I have for years. I trade some of it on the black market, but most of it goes directly to sick people who need it."

"A likely story." The Major smiled indulgently. "But we'll soon have the truth out of you."

"I'm not sure you'd recognize Truth if it ran out from under your mother's porch and bit you," Bear said. "Seems to be a common trait among the religious."

"No need to be abusive, Mr. Bear. Just tell us the truth."

"I just did. I make it. It's not that hard if you know what you're doing. You grow mold on old bread or fruit, then you purify it, then you preserve it with small amounts of relatively common chemicals. You can have the recipe if you want—it's back at the biology lab. It's a bit too complicated to keep in my head."

"Hmm." Major Diamond considered. "Your story might be true. Then again, it might not. Perhaps we'd better inspect your biology lab for ourselves and verify your claims. Or not."

"I'll be happy to show you around," Bear offered. "I'm not about to start a war with The Loward's Fury. If I may ask, what brought you out of Diablo to our neighborhood? Isn't this a little close to the Johnsonites for comfort?"

"We're not worried about the Johnsonites," the Major assured him. "Their territory stops at the river, anyway."

"You're close enough to the river now to make *them* worry," Bear said. "If they get worried enough, you'll have a full-scale battle on your hands."

The Major smiled beatifically. "And that's exactly what we want." At Bear's surprise, he continued, "We have a new commander, you see. He's called His Holiness, the Most High Quaestor, The Iron Sceptre. He is actively seeking military engagement with the Johnsonites."

"Yeah," Bear said laconically. "Captain Hensley mentioned him. Said something about reporting directly to him?"

"That is correct!" The Major said. "It's a brand-new arrangement." He leaned toward Bear conspiratorially. "You see, until now, any and all military actions of The Loward's Fury have been authorized by The Body."

"The Body?"

"The Earthly Embodiment of the Loward's Righteous Anger. They advise the High Templar, you see. And when some wrongdoing is reported, the Body meets and appoints a Holiness Compliance Committee to decide what needs to be done about it. They, in turn, send The Loward's Fury to correct the problem."

Bear mulled this over, then said, "Sounds to me like a lot of people getting excited over someone eating a boiled egg."

The Major scowled. "It's not just about dietary restrictions, you know. Veganism is a minor part of our faith. They also handle criminal cases, and incidents of sexual immorality, and so forth."

"I hear you people don't have sex in the normal fashion," Bear said. "I'm not clear on the details."

"Our sexual practices are none of your business!" the Major was almost shouting. "It's our business, and nobody else's. The High Templar himself decreed the principles of Holy Reproduction for the maximization of fertility rates." He subsided a bit and shook his head sadly. "Sadly, the Womb of Eve is shriveled with sin these days. Our rituals are designed to improve the chances of pregnancy in all fertile females. And it works, too! Our birth rates are far higher than the general population's."

"I'll just bet they are," Bear said. "Including fourteen-year-old girls who don't even know what's happening to them, right? That doesn't sound holy to me—that sounds downright evil."

"You will refrain from blasphemy in my presence!" the Major screamed. "Or I'll have you disciplined."

"I apologize," Bear said. "I did not realize that it was blasphemy. It was merely what I had been led to believe. I'd like to hear the rest of what you were saying about how The Loward's Own are governed. There's been a change, is that it?"

"Yes. Our new movement doesn't contradict any of the old ways. Rather, it compliments them. His Holiness, The Most High Quaestor, The Iron Sceptre, guides us directly without the need for divine revelation."

"Sounds serious," Bear observed.

"It *is* serious," the Major agreed. "We are the strongest and boldest of the Loward's Own. Unlike the former Loward's Angels, who strictly concerned themselves with internal matters, the Loward's Fury directs their attention outward, toward those who are not of The Loward's Own."

"You're talking about the Johnsonites," Bear said.

"Not just the Johnsonites—the Scavs, the Traders, anyone who threatens the well-being of The Loward's Own. In the process, we acquire additional territory for The Loward's Own and also source material goods for the benefit of our people."

"Historically," Bear said, "such warriors are known as bandits, raiders, and invaders. Or pirates. The Vikings had similar ideas."

"I warned you about blasphemy. My patience is at an end. Once more, and I'll have you punished. I guarantee you won't enjoy it."

Bear sighed. "Okay, Major, I think I get the picture. You want my penicillin. I'm willing to give it to you. I'll even show you how to make it. There's no great secret, as I said. It does take some specialized equipment, but there's some in my laboratory you can have, and I'm sure you can find or make more. Will that satisfy you?"

"It's a start," the major said. "A report of the procedure will be conveyed to the Iron Sceptre. He'll decide when he's satisfied." He called out to the guards in the hall, "Have this man chained and prepared for transport. We leave immediately."

"There's just one thing, Major," Bear said. "Making penicillin is a two-man job. I'm going to need my lab assistant."

"Nonsense," the major replied. "One of my men can assist you."

"Well, it's up to you," Bear said, "but I've lost more batches of penicillin to inept assistants than anything else. Still, if you're willing to risk it, I'll do the best I can."

The major thought this over. "Which one is your assistant?"

"The skinny blond," Bear said. "I've just about got her trained perfectly now."

"If you're trying to pull something…"

"Oh, surely, Major, you're not afraid of a little girl, are you? I'll vouch for her conduct."

"You'll vouch? Who are you to vouch?"

"Look—all I'm saying is that there's a right way and wrong way to make penicillin. Whatever you decide, I'll do my best. But we have a much better chance of success with another pair of skilled hands."

"I suppose it couldn't hurt," the major said. Then to the guards, "Go fetch the little blond girl. Chain her up, too."

"Yes, sir." The guards vanished, then reappeared a couple of minutes later with Rosie. She looked absurd in the chains.

"I'm okay," she said to Bear, who was looking her over anxiously. "They fed us. Everyone's fine."

"Among other things," the major said, "she'll serve as a guarantee of your good conduct."

Two soldiers appeared and began putting the chains back on Bear's wrists and ankles. Bear cooperated without protest. "Oh, Major," Bear asked, "what about my other kids?"

"They're no longer your concern. They belong to The Loward's Fury now."

Bear didn't like the sound of that, but he held his peace for the time being.

— Chapter 16 —

Seasons Change

They marched Bear and Rosie back out the way he'd come in, leg chains dragging on the old wooden floor. At the door to the outer courtyard, a young woman in a white lab coat met them and, without a word, emptied a syringe into Rosie's neck. Before Bear could protest, she stuck a second syringe into Bear's neck. Bear looked momentarily surprised, then rolled up his eyes and collapsed into a heap on the floor.

He came to his senses slowly, lying on the couch in the principal's office of his high school. His chains were gone. He opened his eyes a crack. Rosie appeared to be asleep on the other couch. He closed his eyes again and listened for a little while. There wasn't much to hear, just the voices of a pair of sentries of The Fury who had been left there to watch him.

Eventually, there was a commotion in the courtyard, and in came Major Diamond with a half-dozen soldiers. More soldiers remained in the courtyard. Diamond looked Bear over, then turned to one of the sentries. "Well?"

"He's still out, Major," the sentry said. "No sign of—"

Bear groaned faintly.

"Sounds like he's waking up now," the sentry said uselessly.

"Well, wake him up the rest of the way," Major Diamond barked. "Go on, hurry up, get on with it! We haven't got all night!"

The sentry shook Bear gently. "Wake up!" When Bear failed to respond, the sentry shook him even harder. "Wake up, old man! The Major wants a word with you."

Bear groaned again, but didn't speak.

"Move aside, you ninny!" the Major growled. He lashed Bear savagely across the jaw with the back of his hand. "I know you're conscious, so you might as well answer me."

Bear remained motionless. The Major drew back his hand and swung again. This time, Bear caught the Major's hand in mid-swing and held it motionless in his own huge paw. With his other hand, the Major drew his sidearm and placed the barrel against Bear's forehead. Bear released his grip.

"Good choice," the Major said, sneering. "You're not so tough in the face of superior military strength. Will you behave, or shall I have the men cuff you again? Or maybe I'll discipline your little assistant here. Rosie, her name is?"

Rosie groaned and sat up. "Someone call me?" she asked, her voice thick with sleep.

"I'll behave," Bear said, "for now, anyway."

"You'd better," the Major advised. "You won't like what happens if you don't."

"Why?" Bear asked. "What's going to happen?"

"I'll tell you *exactly* what's going to happen. These men are going to escort you two to your 'laboratory,' whatever that is, and you're going to substantiate your claim that you make your own penicillin."

"Uh-huh," Bear said, unimpressed. "And if I can't?"

"You'll be tortured until you can, or until you reveal your sources."

"Right," Bear said. "That's fine. And who's going to judge? These ignorant savages?" He gestured at the soldiers.

"I am," the Major said, ignoring the slur. "I'll personally be your judge, and maybe your executioner. After all, if you can't make medicine, what use are you, you hairy old lard bucket? You're a waste of humanity."

Bear appraised the Major, then said, "Right. So, what are we waiting for? Let's do this." He rose and stumbled out the door, followed by Rosie, prodded along by the guards and Major Diamond. Bear led them down the corridor to the high school's ancient biology lab. After fumbling for the key, he entered and turned on the lights.

"Phew! What a stink!" Major Diamond exclaimed. He took a large flowered bandanna from his trouser pocket and held it over his nose. "Well? Where's the penicillin factory?"

Bear led the men to the west wall of the former classroom. Dozens of jars, vials, flasks, and petri dishes filled the shelves above a long, black-topped counter covered with all manner of glassware mounted on racks and connected with an assortment of rubber tubes.

The Major looked it all over, then turned on Bear. "How stupid do you think we are? Just because we're religious doesn't mean we're idiots. There's nothing here to make medicine out of—it's just a bunch of old junk and jars of mold. You can't fool us that easily."

"Exactly what," asked Bear, "do you think penicillin is made of?" He took a petri dish from the shelves and held it up for the Major to see. Three large blooms of blue-green mold filled the little glass dish. "See that? Do you know what that is? That's Penicillium Rubens. Otherwise known as Penicillium mold. Would you care to take a guess at what I make from the Penicillium mold? Penicillin, the antibiotic, that's what. Yes, I think you're stupid! You're a bunch of idiots. There's Capital-T Truth staring you right in the face and you're all too stupid to recognize it."

The Major backhanded Bear a second time. "Mind your manners. I won't tell you again."

"That's the second time you've hit me, Major," Bear said in a low voice. "If you hit me a third time, I'll kill you."

"Let's see you make some antibiotic, Mr. Bear. Just make some, show us how it's done. *Then* we'll believe you. We'd have to, right?"

"Rosie," Bear said, "go ahead and get your equipment set up."

Rosie looked puzzled. Bear shrugged almost imperceptibly. "Your stuff's under the counter. Get moving."

Rosie began retrieving equipment randomly and arranging it on the counter.

"It's not that simple, Major," Bear explained. "There are four steps involved. First, you have to grow the mold. Then you separate the penicillin from the mold. Then you have to purify it. Then you add preservatives and bottle it."

"Very well. Proceed."

"If you insist. It takes some time, you know. But you're welcome to watch. I suggest you move a few of those metal stools about halfway across the room." Bear graciously helped them arrange the stools and get comfortable. "You'll be able to see everything we do, but you won't be breathing in the harmful mold vapors. Right? Good, yes, just like that."

The Major backhanded Bear once more. "Stop stalling! Get moving! I want to see some action."

Bear gave the Major a long, slow, penetrating look. "I warned you," he said, much too quietly.

"Never mind that nonsense! Get over there and get it done." The major took his automatic pistol from his belt holster and aimed it at Bear's face.

Bear returned to his spot near the glassware on the counter. From below the counter, Bear produced a pair of gas masks. "These will protect Rosie and me from the vapors. Don't worry, they won't reach you." He handed Rosie a mask, helped her strap it on, then donned his own mask. Next, he fiddled with some switches and knobs on a control panel, then waited.

"Well?"

"Just another brief moment, Major. I'm starting the ventilators."

A dense vapor began pouring out of the ceiling vents throughout the laboratory. The Major and the others were momentarily stunned, then the Major yelled, "Gas! Get out of here." He and his men rushed for the door, but it was locked, with no apparent mechanism to unlock it.

It was too late, anyway. The Major lost consciousness and fell to the floor. Forty seconds later, he and his men were dead.

Bear gave it another minute to be sure, then reversed the room's ventilation system. A minute later, the room was free of the lethal gas. Bear removed his gas mask and Rosie's and replaced them under the counter. As he stepped over Major Diamond's lifeless corpse on his way out the door, he looked down at the Major's face. "Told you," he said quietly, and left the room, Rosie right behind him. Bear smiled at his assistant. "That's not the first time someone has invaded our laboratory. You were a great assistant, by the way."

"You killed them all," she said.

"I sure did," Bear replied. "But they started it. No one asked them to come here."

"I guess," Rosie said. "Uh-oh!"

A group of six soldiers was coming up the corridor. "What are you doing out here by yourself?" the squad leader asked Bear. "You're supposed to be making penicillin for the Major."

"We are," Bear said, "but she and I both needed to use the—" He indicated the restroom. "We're all done now. Come with me, I'll take you to the Major." Instead, however, he led them to his private room in the J wing and unlocked the door. "After you, boys," he said, politely holding the door open for them. When they were all inside, Bear softly called the dogs. "Intruders," he intoned quietly. "Kill."

Bruno and Molly lunged at the young soldiers, snarling, biting, ripping. Bear swatted the soldier closest to him, then snatched the soldier's assault rifle as he dropped to the hard tile floor. Without hurrying, while Rosie looked on, surprised, Bear worked the slide on the weapon, set it to burst fire, and methodically started killing each of the soldiers.

Rosie shook off her momentary paralysis, picked up a rifle, and followed Bear's example, aiming deliberately.

Bear had to aim carefully at the last two, because the dogs had them down on the ground, worrying them like rats. It wouldn't do to accidentally injure a dog.

Rosie aimed carefully and dispatched Molly's victim.

Just before Bear shot the last one, the soldier finally worked his sidearm free from its holster and shot Bruno right through the forehead.

Poor Bruno dropped like a stone. Molly whined and licked Bruno's face, but to no avail. Bear gave Bruno a last pat on the head. "Well done, old boy. Thank you. I'll see to it that you're buried properly, if I can." He started down the corridor to the auto shop.

Rosie knelt by Bruno's side and gave him a last farewell pat. "Good doggie," she said. "You did well." Then she ran after Bear.

Bear unlocked the door of the auto shop, hit the button to activate the roll-up doors, then opened the back door of the Bradley. "Load up, Molly." Molly jumped into the passenger compartment without hesitation. Bear and Rosie crawled in after her, then Bear made his way to the gunner's station while the rear ramp closed.

Another squad of Loward's Fury was coming in through the auto shop's front door. Bear unlimbered the Bradley's machine gun and cut them down. He tried to remember how many men that idiot, Diamond, had brought with him, but he had no idea, having been unconscious at the time. *Oh, well, I guess we'll find out.*

He stuffed himself into the commander's hatch, directed Rosie into the gunner's hatch, then eased the Bradley out the bay doors into the night. He steered around to the camouflaged gate, felt for his remote opener, but he didn't have it. Diamond must have taken it. No problem—he just kept rolling. The Bradley went over the chain-link gate as though it weren't there.

He stopped when the Bradley was abreast of the main entrance to the school, then rotated the turret until it was pointing at the front gate. While Rosie observed carefully, one, two, three shots with the Bradley's main gun, and no more entranceway!

Next, he took the Bradley into the school compound. He put a couple of rounds into the administration wing, just for good measure. One young soldier came running up to the tank, arms in the air, shouting, "Don't shoot! Don't shoot! I surrender! Please, I don't want to die!"

"Great, a prisoner is all we need right now." He activated the external megaphone. "Put your weapons on the ground, then come around to the back door. I'll open the hatch. Try anything at all, and I'll shoot you."

"Okay." The soldier put down his rifle, then his pistol, then his combat knife.

Bear opened the back hatch. The soldier entered. Bear spun him around, zip-tied his wrists, put a loop of rope around his feet, then tossed it over a ceiling hook. "Sit down," Bear said, and closed the back hatch.

"What?"

"Too late." Bear pulled the rope until the soldier was hanging by his feet from the top of the passenger compartment, swinging back and forth. "Molly, watch him." Molly sat next to the soldier and sniffed his face. Then, to the soldier, "A single command from me, or any threatening move from you, and this dog will tear you apart. Do I need to explain which body part I trained her to start with?"

"N-n-no, sir. I get it."

"Good," Bear said. "You and I are going to have a nice little chat on our road trip tonight. First question: how many of you are still alive here?"

"What? I mean, I don't know, sir?"

"Well, this conversation isn't going very well, is it? Molly!"

Molly leaped to her feet, growling, and walked stiff-legged toward the upside-down soldier.

"No! Wait! I'll tell you anything I can! Please, sir!"

"Molly." Molly returned to guard position.

"And don't call me 'sir.' I'm Bear."

"Yes, Bear, sir."

"Just 'Bear'."

"Yes, Bear."

"Now, let's try again. "How many of you are still alive?"

"I'm really not certain, s—er, Bear."

"Guess. Try really hard."

"Okay. Um… first the Major went with you to see you make penicillin."

"Right."

"When you didn't come back, the sergeant took a squad to go looking."

"Right."

"The third squad left shortly after them."

"Right."

"The fourth squad was in the administration office. The one you just blew up."

"And you? Where did you come from?"

"Restroom."

"Lucky you. Maybe. What's your name, private?"

"Um… Billy."

"Okay, Billy. You and I are going to take a little road trip together. How would you like that?"

"Um… do I have to ride upside-down, Bear?"

"For now. Later on, we'll have to see. First, though, I have to say goodbye to a friend of mine. An old and dear friend." He drove the Bradley well outside the high-school compound and parked it. Next, he located a rather large remote detonation device in a compartment near the weapons storage. "Goodbye, old friend. Goodbye, Bruno!" Then he turned the handle on the remote. In a tremendous, roaring explosion, the entire high-school compound broke loose from its foundations, and in slow motion settled to the ground. A great cloud of dust and smoke roiled into the night sky. Bear watched for a last, long moment, then closed the hatch behind him and returned to Billy.

"I hated to do that," Bear told the inverted soldier. "I've lived there for almost forty years. My wife and children are buried there. And it's *your fault*! You and the rest of that pack of idiots you call The Fury."

Billy was weeping freely. "I'm sorry, Bear. I truly am. I didn't know what kind of people they were when I joined. I never wanted anything bad to happen to anyone, I swear to the Loward."

Bear studied the young soldier. *Isn't peculiar that his tears are running up his face.*

Bear instructed Rosie to return to the gunner's hatch. Then, he ascended to the commander's hatch and showed her how to use the machine gun. "Just aim and shoot," he told her. He got the Bradley pointed and moved out smartly. "I'm going to miss that place, Rosie Girl. It's been a good home. But… seasons change—it was never meant to last forever. It's a miracle it lasted as long as it did."

— Chapter 17 —

My Friend Brad

Bear got the Bradley going south along the front edge of his former home. He plowed right on through the intersection, continuing southward. The Bradley would do nearly forty miles per hour, but he kept a steady pace of around five miles per hour. They had only two miles to go tonight, and quietness and stealth were key to the operation, rather than speed.

As soon as the Bradley was trundling along in the right direction, Bear said to Rosie. "How are you doing?"

"All right, so far," Rosie said, "but it's only been three minutes." She smiled.

"How are you doing with the machine gun?" Bear asked. "Think you'll be able to aim it?"

Rosie swiveled the gun from side to side on its pintle and tried aiming at various random objects. "I think so. I guess we'll find out. How about the big gun, Mr. The Bear? Are we going to be using that tonight?"

"Maybe," Bear said. "We'll have to see how things work out. Did you figure out how to use it?"

"Partly. This thingie makes it go up and down, and this stick here makes the whole turret move from side to side."

"That's right," Bear said. "You've got the idea. And when you get the big gun pointed, you use this button to fire a shell."

"A shell?"

"Explosive shell. It's like a bullet, only bigger, and it blows up. It's for use against vehicles and buildings. It's overkill against foot soldiers. This selects single fire or three-round bursts."

"Same as the assault rifle?"

"Exactly."

"Right." Rosie studied Bear's face. "How about you, Mr. The Bear? How are you doing? That was quite a thing you did back there."

"You can say that again," Bear said. "I've lost three kids, my home of thirty-five years, a car, a wonderful dog, and killed several dozen young religious fanatics. And the night's not over yet."

"Are you sad? They didn't give you a lot of choice."

"I know. Still, it's like I told you yesterday: it's a heavy thing to take a human life. Especially young, stupid ones who don't even understand what's going on. It was the same in the War." He sighed. "And I'm afraid there are going to be lots more of them before we're done."

"My parents are kind of dumb, but they're not bad. The Loward's Own isn't bad, either—they try to teach us to be good. But these Loward's Fury soldiers just start shooting." She brooded over that, then said, "We really need to find Echo and the boys."

"That's the idea," Bear agreed. "But I'm afraid it's going to get rough. You shot one soldier. How does that feel? Are you willing to kill many more for your new friends?"

Rosie's face took on a grim aspect. "I don't know."

"Well, you'd better figure it out pretty quick. I won't think less of you if you can't do it, but I need to know."

Rosie nodded soberly.

They turned left, eastward, at the next major intersection, which put them in a straight line toward their destination. Bear pointed to the orange glow of the approaching dawn lining the tops of the enormous mountain range far to the east. "Look at that, Rosie Girl. The sun's coming up already. No wonder I'm so tired. Hey—did you see something moving up ahead?"

They peered into the misty gray dawn. Sure enough, shadows were moving along the edges of the road, in the ditches, behind trees, crouching by piles of wreckage and detritus. Bear eased the Bradley to a halt and waited. A series of whistle signals ran down the line from Bear's position eastward. A few minutes later, a man carrying an assault rifle approached the Bradley, accompanied by two others. They weren't wearing uniforms, although the one with the assault rifle had captain's bars on his baseball cap. He approached Bear cautiously, hands extended from his sides to show he was not aggressive.

"Good morning, sir, miss. I'm Captain Skeeter, of the Third Division of Johnson's Militia. Mind if I ask who you are, and where you're headed?"

"Name's Bear. This is Miss Rose. I live a few big blocks away, to the north and west, in an old high school. Or I did, anyway, until today. And I'm headed for that little church a quarter-mile down the road."

"Care to share your mission? No offense intended."

"And none taken, Captain. Those religious nuts have three of my kids. I aim to get them back."

"Boys or girls?" the Captain asked.

"One girl, two boys. Why, does it matter?"

"It might. Were they wearing blue uniforms, the religious nuts? With silver angels on them?"

"Sure were."

"That the Loward's Fury," the Captain explained. "They're supposedly a branch of the Loward's Own, but they're not."

"So I've heard," Bear said.

"The Loward's Own are stupid, but basically harmless. They're busy starving themselves to death out in the old Diablo district. Johnson calls it a 'self-limiting problem.' The Loward's Fury is something else altogether. They have rituals, and some of those rituals involve some very vicious practices."

"You mean the sex and fertility rites?"

"And worse," the Captain said. He took a few steps toward Bear and lowered his voice. "I've heard they eat the dead. I can't verify it, though. Still."

"So you're Johnsonites, I take it?"

"We are."

"And may I ask your mission?"

"We've had reports that the Loward's Fury was making advances into what we consider our territory, even though we don't occupy it at this time. Our job was recon, with an option to engage if circumstances warrant."

"And do they?" Bear asked.

"Do circumstances warrant?" The Captain rubbed his chin. "Depends on how you look at it."

"What do you mean?"

"Well, sir, ordinarily we don't discuss our operations outside our individual units. However, in view of your missing children…"

"What about them?"

"It's not obvious from here," the Captain explained, "but this is a pretty big operation. Johnson has been increasingly concerned about The Fury—there's no other way to put it, Mr. Bear—"

"Just 'Bear.'"

"Got it. Well, there's no other way to put it, but The Fury are just plain bad people. Their head honcho, goes by the name of Iron Sceptre, or somesuch nonsense, is, by all reports, the embodiment of pure evil. We have heard he gets off by skinning his victims alive over a period of days or weeks while violating them in various ways."

"I see," Bear said through clenched jaws. A muscle in his cheek began twitching. "Not good."

"It gets worse. Before we rendezvoused here, we made several sweeping patrols of the area. One of them encountered a small group of The Fury with a transport wagon. Our guys killed the entire group and seized the wagon. There were two kids in it—two boys, no girls. One of the boys was in pretty bad shape, missing a few toes, it seems. Our medic says he'll be okay, but he's going to walk funny for the rest of his life."

"What about the girl?"

"The other boy, name of Rat, said they took the girl in a different wagon, and possibly in a different direction. Which would make sense. We have intelligence that The Fury has a defensible position on our side of the river, upstream a bit, a kind of temple."

"Temple?"

"Sorry, Bear, that's all we know so far. Our patrol questioned the troops with the wagons, briefly. They also mentioned this church here as a new outpost. Further questioning suggested that they plan to annex an old high school that wasn't completely destroyed during the War. Said some old hairy fellow lives there all alone, and would be an easy target."

Bear smiled grimly.

"I take it he was wrong about the easy target?"

"Dead wrong," Bear said.

It was the Captain's turn to grin.

"And you don't have to worry about them taking over the high school. It no longer exists."

"I see," said the Captain. "I'm sorry to hear that."

"It was inevitable," Bear said. "I'm surprised it lasted as long as it did."

"Body count?"

"About three dozen uniformed soldiers of various ranks, plus a nasty piece of work named Major Diamond. A real horse's backside."

The Captain's eyebrows shot up. "I know of him. He's on our kill list."

"You can cross him off now."

"I see. Plus three dozen of his men, eh? All by yourself?"

"Not quite. Miss Rose was with me, and I lost a good dog. Still have Molly, here."

When Molly heard her name, she stuck her head up through the hatch and sniffed the brisk morning air.

"Hi, Molly," The Captain said. "Good girl!"

Bear nodded his approval. "And, of course, there's my friend Brad."

"Brad?"

Bear patted the armor plate near the hatch. "Short for 'Bradley Fighting Vehicle.'"

The Captain gave a low, approving whistle. "She's some kind of tank. Borrowed from the war, I presume?"

Bear and the Captain laughed together. "Exactly, Captain. They weren't using it anymore. She's been on ice at the high school since just after the War. I've kept her clean and maintained, and twice a year I've run her up in the shop. I didn't see any point in leaving her in the ruins of the school. More to the point, she helped create some of the ruins of the school."

"I don't doubt it," The Captain said, eyeing the Bradley enviously. "Just wish we had one of our own."

"Well, look at it this way, Captain: we're here, you're here, Brad's here, and The Fury have my kids. You've told me that the kids are no longer at the church."

"As far as we know," the Captain confirmed.

"Then, at this moment in time, for all practical purposes, you do have a Bradley of your own. And Rosie needs some target practice. Would you mind, terribly, if we took a few shots at the church, just for fun? You weren't planning on using it yourselves, were you?"

"No, not at all, Bear. She's all yours."

"Fair enough. If you'd be so kind as to ask your men to step out of the road, I'll just edge the tank a bit closer. Hop on!"

"Sure thing." Captain Skeeter climbed up on the tank next to Bear, cupped his hands around his mouth, and shouted, "Hey, you men! Clear the roadway! On the double!"

As the men moved aside, Bear edged the Bradley forward until he felt that the church would be an easy target. "Okay, Rosie Girl. Let's see if you can line up the crosshairs of the reticle on the church."

Rosie tentatively manipulated both the main gun and the turret until the church appeared centered behind the crosshairs.

"Good," Bear said. "I think you've got it." He turned to Captain Skeeter. "Maybe alert your men to look for people leaving the church?"

"Prepare to fire on all personnel leaving the church!" he called. His men came to order and readied their weapons. He nodded at Bear.

"Okay, Rosie, make sure it's set for burst fire and give it a go."

Rosie did.

Thoop! Thoop! Thoop! Away went the 25mm rounds. They struck the church dead center, just below the steeple. At first, nothing seemed to happen, but then the church toppled in slow motion.

"Good shot," Bear said. "I'll pull up a bit to give you a shot at the utility buildings around back."

As Bear started the Bradley forward, dozens of Loward's Fury soldiers came running out of the church, which was now burning furiously. Captain Skeeter's men were picking them off. They were excellent shots, Bear noted—one shot, one kill.

When the long flank of the church was exposed, Bear said, "Okay, Rosie. All yours. Bring it down."

Rosie brought the broad side of the church into the crosshairs, and without waiting for Bear's okay, hit the firing button.

Thoop! Thoop! Thoop! The entire flank of the church collapsed in a maelstrom of smoke and flame. Many more soldiers were fleeing the burning buildings, a fair number of them firing at the Militiamen.

"Machine gun time, Rosie," Bear suggested.

Rosie left the main gun's targeting system and nestled her shoulder into the butt of the machine gun's stock. And then… nothing.

"What's the matter, Rosie?" Bear asked.

"I… I… can't."

"It's okay," Bear said. "It's normal to choke during your first firefight."

"I didn't choke back at the school," Rosie said. "But that was… different, somehow."

By this time, bullets were pinging off the armor of the Bradley. One of them struck close to Rosie, then bounced off and grazed her arm, leaving a bright red streak. "Hey!" Rosie exclaimed. Another round pinged off the Bradley and whizzed by her ear. "Hey," she said again, indignantly, "they're shooting at *me!*"

"They are at that," Bear agreed.

Another round zinged by like an angry hornet, causing Molly, who had just stuck her nose out the hatch to see what all the commotion was about, to yelp.

"They can't do that!" Rosie shouted. "Leave my dog alone!" She tightened her grip on the machine gun and squeezed the trigger. In moments, not one of the Loward's Fury remained standing. Rosie just kept on firing.

Bear put his hand on her shoulder. "Enough. You can stop now. They're all dead." When Rosie failed to respond, Bear shook her gently. "Rosie, stop firing! They're are all dead now. Stop, do you hear?"

Reluctantly, Rosie released her grip on the machine gun and surveyed the field. "I… I… I killed them *all*." She was shaking from head to toe.

Bear eased her hands off the machine gun and held her close. "You sure did, Kiddo."

Bear held her until she stopped shaking and had finished crying, for the moment. "I see what you meant, now, Mr. The Bear, about taking lives being a heavy thing."

Bear nodded. "Yes."

"But they were shooting at us."

"Yes, they were."

"We blew up their church."

"We did that," Bear agreed softly.

"I wish… I wish…"

"I know, Rosie. I wish, too. Sometimes that's all there is."

Captain Skeeter gave Rosie a tentative pat on the shoulder. "We do what has to be done. You did well. They were bad people, and they would have killed you, killed us all, without a second thought. As unpleasant as it was, it needed doing. Speaking of which, we can't begin to guess what they're doing to your friends right now."

"Good thought," Bear said. "What do you say we gather ourselves and pay a little social call on our religious friends in their nice new temple?" He pointed northwest.

"Sounds good to me, Bear. Let me get my men started moving. Hey! Hank! Step over here for a moment, would you please?"

The Bear and The Rose

— Chapter 18 —

Billy

Apleasant-looking young fellow carrying a pre-War hunting rifle with an expensive scope trotted up. "Yes, sir?"

"I want you to meet Bear and Miss Rose. They're the ones responsible for the sudden disappearance of one local church. Bear, Miss Rose, this is my second-in-command, Hank."

They shook hands all around. Captain Skeeter continued, "Bear has offered their services and those of his friend, Brad."

Hank looked around, then at the Captain, eyebrows raised.

Captain Skeeter laughed and patted the Bradley's metal plating. "This is Brad, short for Bradley Fighting Vehicle. It's from the War, before you were born, Hank."

"Well, that's mighty kind of you, Mr. Bear."

"Just 'Bear' is fine."

"Okay, 'Bear' it is, then," Hank acknowledged. "I have to say, I'm real pleased that you're joining up with us."

"It's not quite like that," Captain Skeeter said. "The two boys you picked up are Bear's kids. And, more to the point, the girl that you didn't pick up is also Bear's kid."

Bear said, "Brad and Rosie and I will go along with you to try to recover my kids. After that, we'll have to see what happens."

"I get it," Hank said. "Sounds great to me. I have to say, you sure saved us a lot of trouble taking that church down. Saved a lot of our guys' lives, too, I shouldn't wonder."

Rosie brightened a little at that.

Hank said, "So, what can I do for you, Captain? Are we going to the Fury's temple now?"

"If I may," Bear interjected, "there are a couple of minor issues I'd like to discuss before we roll."

"Certainly, sir," Skeeter said. "Hang on just a moment, if you don't mind. Hank, give the order to prepare to move out. Have the men break camp and pack up."

"Yes, sir. Burial detail?"

"Don't bother," Captain Skeeter said. "Crows have to eat, too, just like worms. You can leave that scum for the birds. Come right back here, when you're done giving orders."

"Yes, sir." Hank took off, double time, toward the smoldering ruins of the church where the men were milling about. In moments, the entire site was buzzing like a beehive as the men put things in order for departure. Hank was back in a flash. "The men will be ready in a few minutes, sir."

"Right. Good work, Hank. Now, Bear, what's on your mind?"

"Couple of things," Bear said. "First of all, there's a young fellow inside this thing who needs some attention."

"Wounded, you mean?" Captain Skeeter asked.

"Oh, no," Bear said. "Not much anyway. It's more of an orientation issue. He's the last survivor of The Fury's assault on my high school—my home, you see—and he's, well, he's upside down."

"I don't understand," the Captain said.

"Come on in, I'll show you. I suppose you'd like a look inside, anyway."

The Captain and Hank grinned. "Sure would, sir," Hank said.

"Just 'Bear,' please, son. Go on around back. I'll drop the hatch so you can get in." Bear's head and shoulders disappeared from the commander's hatch.

Captain Skeeter and Hank climbed in through the back hatch. There was room for six soldiers to sit in the passenger compartment, but Bear's presence made the interior seem minuscule.

"Here's the fellow I was telling you about," Bear said. "He's been here for a while. Probably pretty uncomfortable by now. And almost certainly has to use—no, he doesn't, he's peed himself. Not surprising, under the circumstances, but what a mess! We're going to have to hose this thing out." He elbowed the kid in his inverted rib cage. "Couldn't hold it just a while longer? Shame on you." He sighed. "Kids these days, honestly." When Bear took the combat knife from his belt, the upside-down kid totally lost it. He screamed and thrashed and hollered and choked. Bear looked on, completely disgusted. "Oh, for—" With one swift motion he cut the kid down. The kid landed in a heap in the puddle of his own urine. "Help me get him out of here, would you please?"

Bear, Captain Skeeter, and Hank dragged the kid out the back hatch unceremoniously. The kid lay in the grass by the side of the road, weeping hysterically as the three men looked on.

Bear said, "It had been in my mind that you could question him, but by the looks of him, that's not going to work out. Too bad."

"Seems unlikely he knows anything of value," Captain Skeeter said. He walked over to the crying, writhing boy and pulled his sidearm from his belt. "I hate to do it," he said. "He's just a kid." He worked the slide on the pistol.

"He was in the can when I eliminated the rest of his crew," Bear explained. "Seems a shame to waste him. Any chance you could rehabilitate him? Bring him to his senses?"

"We've tried in the past," Captain Skeeter said. "But by the time we get them, they've been brainwashed beyond salvaging. I don't know what they do to them in that place, but they're not rational beings anymore." He took aim.

"Wait, please, Captain Skeeter," Rosie said. She had climbed out of the gunner's hatch and come around to the back of the tank. She knelt by the weeping boy's head. "What's your name, boy? Can you tell me your name?"

"B… B… Billy."

"Billy. That's a nice name." She brushed the hair from his eyes. "Well, Billy, these men don't really want to hurt you. In fact, they would help you, if you'd let them."

The boy's weeping subsided to a whimper. Rosie continued, "But you'll have to do something in return. You'll have to listen to everything they tell you, and try as hard as you can to learn from them. Can you do that? For me?"

Billy nodded.

Rosie looked up at Captain Skeeter. "Captain?"

Captain Skeeter looked dubious.

Bear said, "Captain Skeeter, perhaps as a favor to both of us?"

Captain Skeeter squeezed his eyes tight and held them closed for a long moment. Then he reluctantly put his pistol back in its holster. "All right. As a favor to you, then. I'll treat him as a military prisoner for now, but after the assault, you'll have to take charge of him."

"Thank you," Bear said. "We will."

Molly sniffed around the boy, who was now motionless and quiet on the grass. She tentatively licked his tear-stained face. Billy smiled, just a little.

Hank issued a brisk order and two Militiamen came and carried the boy off.

Bear realized he'd been holding his breath, so he let it out and started breathing normally again. When had he become so tenderhearted? Only hours ago, he'd killed maybe thirty boys just like this one. He shook his head, wondering if he was going soft in his old age.

"What else did you want to discuss?" Captain Skeeter asked.

"I noticed that quite a few of your men are not that well equipped."

"We do the best we can. Most of them brought their own firearms from home."

Hank added, "This here hunting rifle has been in my family for generations. It has served us well."

Bear nodded. "I don't doubt it. That's a fine old scope."

Captain Skeeter continued, "A few of us have military-grade weapons, like me." He displayed his assault rifle for Bear's inspection. "Mostly, though, the men pack whatever they have. We're not a real militia, you see. We don't even have uniforms. Johnson is adamant that the Johnsonites should never have a standing army. He says we'll defend our homes and our families, but we'll never take territory by force. And he preaches that every man has the right and responsibility to defend his own community. But we're not professional soldiers, and we don't want to be."

"I see," Bear said. "I didn't know this about the Johnsonites."

"Johnson wants us to be self-sufficient and take care of ourselves and each other, and help as many others as we can," Hank said. "But he's not a religious leader. He's not really even a community leader, officially—we have a Mayor and a Town Council and all the rest—Johnson is just a good man with some good ideas, and he's helping people to build new lives. Sometimes he tells stories about another militia from long before the War. He calls them 'Minutemen' and says they could be ready to defend themselves in a single minute. But they weren't professional soldiers, either. Johnson wants us to be like that, I think."

"Very interesting," Bear said. "All new information to me. This Johnson guy seems like a fellow I'd like to meet sometime."

"It isn't hard to meet him. He's just a guy. Hangs out in a restaurant in Old Town. Anybody can walk in and talk to him whenever they want."

"Well, look," Bear said, "the reason I asked about the weapons is that I know where there's a cache of some military-grade weapons available for the taking. They're in good shape—I know because they're mine. At the moment, they're buried in the rubble of my high school, but I'm sure your guys could dig them out in no time. They're all locked up in a sealed steel cabinet I had hidden in the wall. I'd like to keep a few of them for myself, but the rest of them are yours if you want them."

"Absolutely, we want them. Can we swing by there on the way to the Temple?"

"That's what I was thinking," Bear said. "I'll show your guys where to look. I'm sure Major Diamond and the Loward's Fury didn't have time to locate them, so they're all probably intact if the blast didn't damage them."

"That's very generous of you, Bear," Captain Skeeter said. "I'm not sure how we could repay you."

"I'm not looking for repayment. I'm interested in just one thing—getting my girl back before something unspeakable happens to her. If military-grade weapons make our assault on the Temple more likely to be successful, I'm all for it."

"Fair enough," Captain Skeeter said. "I'll have Hank prepare for a minor excavation. What's next?"

"One more thing: Brad, here, is designed for an operating crew of three, commander, gunner, and driver. I'm okay here in the commander's hatch, and I can drive from here, but I'd rather not. I have a gunner, as you can see, and she's doing just fine."

Rosie nodded and smiled.

"But I'm short a driver. It would be very helpful if we had one. Brad steers a lot like a bulldozer. There are just two levers, one for each track. If you have anyone who can operate heavy machinery, they can probably drive Brad just fine. They don't have to be an expert, only reasonably bright."

Captain Skeeter grinned. "As it happens, I have some considerable experience with a bulldozer. We have one in Old Town that we use mostly for clearing rubble and such. If it's all right with you, I'd like to take a crack at the driver position myself. I'm sure I can command from here. Anyway, Hank does most of the real work. Right, Hank?"

"Sure thing, Skeet. Er, I mean, Captain!"

"Okay," Captain Skeeter said. "While you're at it, pick six of your best close-quarters fighters and get them ready to ride inside the tank with Bear and me, but walking close behind the Bradley for now. The rest of the men can form a column behind them. Convoy speed will be five miles per hour. Our intel says that the so-called Temple is only three miles from here, right across the river. A bit more, counting the detour for the weapons. It's early yet. I'd be a happy man if we could take the temple and rescue the girl before lunch."

"Me, too, Captain, me too," Hank said. "I'm on my way."

"Before you go, Hank," Bear said, "if it's okay with Captain Skeeter, could you have one of your men bring up the little red car I left parked there? It's my shopping cart, and I'd hate to lose it."

"You can't miss it," Rosie said. "It looks like an electric roller skate!"

— Chapter 19 —

Piece of Cake

The column formed up behind the Bradley in relatively short order. There were more men and equipment around the site of the destroyed church than had been apparent. Men and trucks appeared from side roads and from the wrecked school's yard at the intersection. The precision with which they assembled themselves for travel told of many hours of training. Less than ten minutes after Hank gave the order to move out, the entire column was ready to go.

"If you don't mind, Bear," Captain Skeeter said, "I'd like to say a few words to the troops before we start. Do you mind if I hop up on the turret?"

"Help yourself," Bear said. "Here, use this." He handed the Captain the microphone of the Bradley's bullhorn.

The captain climbed up onto the turret and spoke into the microphone. "Listen carefully, men. Just a couple of things: for one, we're going to pay our Loward's Fury friends a visit at their new temple across the river."

Captain Skeeter waited until the men in front had passed the word down the line, then continued. "For another, we're going to make a slight detour to pick up some assault weapons our new friend, Bear, has offered us. So some of you will get better weapons today. Decide among yourselves who needs them most. We don't know yet how many there will be. We'll have to dig for them in the ruins of a high school."

This, too, was passed along the column, and as the men got the message, a muted cheer went up.

"Convoy speed is five miles per hour. Keep a tight formation. Shoot anything that isn't us, in case some of the Loward's Fury are still lurking about. Otherwise, keep it quiet. We've only about five miles to go, total, so we'll be there in a little over an hour. Ready? Let's march!"

Captain Skeeter took his position in the driver's hatch, put the Bradley in gear, and set the speed controls. "Five miles per hour, on the mark," he reported to Bear.

"Good. Steady as she goes. We'll go straight ahead for two large blocks, then turn north. That'll take us straight to the high school."

Bear told Rosie, "You saw how the main gun took that church right down. It will also obliterate any vehicle we're likely to encounter. So, absolutely do not shoot this thing at the buildings until we're sure that Echo is safe. Got it?"

"Got it."

"Good. Use the machine gun until it's time for the big gun. It was in automatic mode at the church, but for now, we'll set it to burst mode. You can switch it back to full automatic if things heat up."

As they approached the ruins of the high school, Captain Skeeter turned into the parking lot, then brought the massive machine to a halt just before the former main entrance, next to Major Diamond's two military troop-transport trucks.

Bear's shopping cart zoomed up and parked alongside the trucks. Two men hopped out and watched the long tendrils of greasy black smoke drift up from the remains of the concrete walls and pillars. "Okay if we leave the little car here, for now?" one of the men asked.

"Okay with me," Captain Skeeter said. "We can come back for it later. Okay, Bear?"

Bear nodded. "Okay with me, Captain. It's your show now. My old armory is somewhere underneath that particular pile of rubble, probably not very deep." He pointed at the ruins of the administration office. "I'm going to step over to the ditch, there, and relieve myself. Old-man bladder, you know. Then I'll wait in the Bradley for your men to get finished."

Captain Skeeter assigned two men to accompany Bear to the ditch. Bear returned to the Bradley and sat on the turret, watching Captain Skeeter's men dig through the ruins. They located the armory and opened it with the code Bear gave them. They distributed the weapons according to some internal priority system: first the assault weapons and SMGs, next the sidearms, then the combat knives. The ammunition was next. In fifteen minutes, they were ready to resume travel.

When Captain Skeeter returned to the Bradley, Bear said, "Those two transports used to belong to Major Diamond, the commandant of the old church outpost."

"Who owns them now?" the Captain asked.

"You do, I suppose."

"Hang on a moment." He located Hank. "Hey, Hank, we're liberating those two trucks. Can you see about drivers and who-all gets to ride in them, or maybe reserve them for some equipment, or whatever?"

"Sure thing, Cap! Gimme a sec to get it done." A few minutes later, Hank called, "All set, Captain. Move out!"

Meanwhile, Captain Skeeter, who had returned to the driver's hatch, was slowly easing the Bradley back around to the road. At the command to move out, he started off southward, back to the thoroughfare, followed by the two transport trucks and the rest of the convoy.

A right turn at the T intersection, a left turn at the next big avenue, and a gentle curve along a broad and spacious former boulevard brought them to the foot of the old iron bridge that crossed the Little River and led the way to Old Town. The captain smoothly brought the Bradley to a halt behind a curtain of trees, where the road began to climb the levee to bridge level.

"Well done!" Bear said. "What happens now?"

"Now, we wait," Captain Skeeter replied.

They didn't have to wait long. Two men on foot ran down the bridge ramp and up to the Bradley. Evidently, the militiamen recognized them, because no one raised an alarm.

"Hey, Hooker, Barrigan. What do we know?"

"A bit more than we did this morning, Cap," Hooker said. "There was a wooden wagon through here early this morning, before dawn. Six men with it, plus the driver. Came up the big boulevard and across the bridge. The guards at the barricade seemed to be expecting it because they waved them right though."

"Could you tell what was inside?" Bear asked. "I'm looking for a teenage girl."

"No, sir," Barrigan reported. "It was an open wagon, but it was covered with a tarp."

Hooker nodded agreement. "Could have been anything or anyone inside, Cap. And no one was talking."

"Okay," Captain Skeeter said. "What else?"

"Well, there's a new gun at the barricade," Hooker said. "It's some kind of old military cannon on wheels. Could be a problem. Also, there's six guards there now, not just two."

"Gunners, maybe?" Captain Skeeter asked. "To go with the cannon?"

Barrigan shrugged. "Could be, hard to say. One thing's for certain, though—we're not just going to waltz across that bridge."

"What do they look like, the guards and the cannon escort?" the Captain asked.

"All Loward's Fury," Hooker said. "All in uniforms. All carrying assault weapons."

Captain Skeeter exchanged a look with Bear, then said, "What about the temple? Anything going on there?"

"No, sir, not really," Hooker said.

"The wagon went up to the back doors," Barrigan added. "A few Furies came out and carried some stuff inside, couldn't see what it was, then the wagon pulled around to the courtyard on the other side of the church building. Don't know what happened to the horses, couldn't see from where we were."

"What about that Iron Sceptre character?" the Captain asked. "Any sign of him? Someone in an unusual uniform, or a robe, or any weird stuff like that?"

"No, sir," Barrigan said. "Not that we saw, anyway."

"One more thing, Captain," Hooker said. "There's some kind of boat tied up at a little concrete landing, a hundred yards or so downstream from the bridge, on the temple side. Didn't see any activity there, though."

"Okay, men," Captain Skeeter said. "Good work. Get yourselves some coffee and some chow, if you can find any. No more scouting today, but be ready to join the main assault."

"Roger that, Captain," Hooker said, and the pair headed for the coffee truck.

Bear accepted a cup of steaming coffee from a militiaman who'd just come up the line. There was one for Rosie and the Captain, too. As they sipped their coffee, the three of them ruminated about the situation. Bear finished his, set the empty cup on the turret. "Well, Captain, what's the plan?"

"As I see it," Captain Skeeter said, "There are three, no, four parts to this operation." He enumerated on his fingers. "First, we have to get across the bridge. Then we have to penetrate the temple. Next, we find the girl and get her out."

"What's the fourth part?" Rosie asked.

"Oh." Captain Skeeter smiled. "That's easy: we burn the building to the ground and kill everyone left in it."

"Ah," Bear said. "That's it? That's all there is to it?" Bear shook his massive head sadly. "Sounds like a big job! What do you think, Molly girl? Can we do it?" He bent down and put his ear next to Molly's perpetually smiling mouth, listened for a moment, then straightened up. "No worries," Bear said. "Molly says, 'Piece of cake!'"

— Chapter 20 —

A Little Social Call

Captain Skeeter laughed, then patted Molly's shaggy head. "Well, if Molly says it's all right…"

Hank walked up. "Hi, Molly. Hi, Cap, Bear, Miss Rose. Column's all set to move on your order. What's the plan?"

"We were just talking about how we're going to go about this little social call of ours," Bear said.

"Well, let's see, now," Hank said. "First step, get that cannon off the bridge. How about we roll up to our end of the bridge, and open fire with the 25mm, keep shooting until they're gone?"

"Hmm… maybe," Bear said, "but I don't really want to damage the bridge. It's pretty old, anyway. If we damage it, we'll have to swim across and do the job without the Bradley. Not optimal, I'd say."

Hank said, "Scouts report the barricade is well back from the bridge itself, up on the levee on the far side, maybe twenty or thirty feet back. I don't think we'll have to worry about the bridge."

"Sounds good," Bear said. "How about this, then: let's put our six men inside the Bradley now, and another, say, twenty-five or so walking behind the Bradley. They can move up as soon as we take out the barricade. We'll roll down the levee into the church's back lot and make our entrance. As soon as we get inside, the rest of the men can advance and surround the church complex on the west and south sides."

"That works," Captain Skeeter said. "Scouts say on the north side of the temple is a ruined apartment complex, so there won't be much activity there. And the east side is the river."

"The river, right," Bear said. "The scouts mentioned a little boat landing. Maybe send a small fire team down to the boat and keep it secure?"

"Good," Captain Skeeter said. "Hank, you'll head up the invasion team with the Bradley. Can you assign the fire team and a commander for the main column? Bring thirty-five of your best close-combat fighters back with you."

"No problem, Cap." In only a few minutes, he was back with three dozen men. "Greg will command the column. Tommy's got the fire team for the boat landing."

Captain Skeeter nodded carefully. "Good men, Greg and Tommy. Well done, Hank."

"Thank you, sir. How do you want my team to proceed?"

"You and five men will get into the Bradley now. The Bradley will roll up to the bridge and take out the barricade. As soon as the barricade is down, the rest of your men will come up behind and follow the Bradley down the levee and into the church. Stick close, use the Bradley for cover, don't take any chances. The Bradley will create an entrance and subdue any initial resistance. Then you and your men will exit the Bradley and form six squads with the thirty-five men for standard mop-up. Go through every room. Kill anything in a uniform—these are Bad People. One word of caution: Bear's teenage girl is probably being held captive in there somewhere. He'd like her back unharmed, if possible. Let's just hope we're not too late. Everyone understand their part?"

Everyone did.

"I forgot to mention: Bear is the Bradley commander. Miss Rose is the gunner. I'm driving. We three *must* stay with the Bradley at all times. We're going in with the hatches closed, but we'll open up as soon as it's safe, okay? Oh—it's all right for your men to ride on the Bradley, as needed. Ready? Let's load up."

Hank and five men ran up the back ramp of the Bradley and got settled. As the Bradley began its ascent of the levee, the rest of the assault team advanced to the edge of the tree line and waited there.

Toogh-toogh-toogh-toogh, up went the Bradley to the top of the ramp. The sight of the monstrous machine miraculously materializing across the river from them momentarily paralyzed the Fury soldiers manning the barricade. A moment later, they exploded into action, two of them working the old artillery piece, the other four firing assault weapons at the Bradley.

Rosie fired a single round dead center into the artillery piece. *Boom!* No more artillery piece. The barricade exploded into a cloud of fiery splinters. There was no sign of the artillerymen. Three of the riflemen were still on their feet and still blasting away at the Bradley.

Captain Skeeter started the Bradley moving, while Rosie used the machine gun to eliminate the riflemen. Back down the hill behind the Bradley, the rest of the assault team was already in motion. They took up their positions in the shelter of the Bradley. The rest of the column began moving up behind them.

Bear and Captain skeeter poked their heads up out of the turret. The old bridge was creaking and groaning.

"I don't like this, Skeeter," Bear said. "If we go into the river, that's the end of it."

Captain Skeeter ordered the thirty-five-man assault team to wait at the entrance to the bridge. The Bradley roared as the Captain ran up the mighty Diesel engine. He released the brakes and the Bradley shot forward across the ancient, rusty, bridge decking.

Bear started breathing again as the Bradley reached the safety of the packed-earth levee. He hadn't realized that he was holding his breath.

Captain Skeeter waved the assault team forward to rejoin the Bradley. As soon as they reassembled, Bear gave the order, and the Bradley rumbled down the levee into the church parking lot.

A few dozen Fury soldiers sallied forth from various portions of the church building and the auxiliary wings. Rosie cut them down with the machine gun. Plus, it seems the six militiamen inside the Bradley had worked out how to use the firing ports. Meanwhile, the rest of the assault team stayed carefully in the safe shadow of the Bradley.

"Hey, Captain," Bear called. "On your way down the levee, did you happen to notice the blue-painted areas of the parking lot?"

"I sure did—on the north side of the church building."

"Take us around there, will you? I have a hunch."

"Sure thing, Bear." He whipped the Bradley around to the north, requiring the assault team to run to keep up.

Rosie remained alert, but no additional soldiers left the church buildings. As they rounded the northeast corner of the church, Bear spotted a row of double glass doors just beyond the blue-painted parking area.

"Take her in, Captain!" Bear yelled. He poked his head out of the hatch and hollered to the assault team. "This is it! Watch yourselves. We're going in!"

Captain Skeeter revved up the Bradley and drove through the glass doors and surrounding structure as though they weren't there. It came away with the aluminum door frames on its broad metal shoulders.

Bear released the back hatch. Hank and his men came roaring out of the Bradley and joined the assault team in attack formation.

On the stage of the church, where the pulpit should have been, something peculiar was happening. A tall man with a long beard wearing a strangely decorated hooded robe was holding a long silver dagger high above his head, chanting quietly, eyes closed. Hundreds of flickering candles ringed the stage.

Beneath him, on a white stone table, a naked female lay unconscious. Her hair hung down to the floor on both sides of the stone table, as did her arms. The tall man lowered the knife slowly, slowly, until the point touched the female's abdomen. He traced a line down from her navel, leaving a trail of bright red blood on her skin.

The moment the Bradley crashed through the wall of glass, the tall man dropped the knife, picked up the naked girl, fled along the south wall, and exited the main hall through a side door.

Bear shouted, "Shoot him!" but it was too late—he was gone in a flash.

Bear lifted his bulk out of the hatch, but Rosie pulled him back. "The three of us stay with the vehicle at all times, remember?" Bear allowed himself to be pulled back to the commander's position. "Yeah, I remember. Hey, Hank! What color was that girl's hair?"

"Brown. Is she yours?"

"I don't know," Bear said. "She was too far away to be sure. Maybe, I hope so. Keep looking!"

"Roger that." Hank and his squad resumed their methodical search, behind the stage, around the altar, and in-between every pew. "Nothing here," Hank reported. "We're going to search the side buildings."

Intermittent firing sounded from the various side rooms and more distant firing from outside. Bear directed Captain Skeeter to take the Bradley back out the way they'd entered, through the remains of the glass doors.

"Ready?" he asked Captain Skeeter once they were outside.

The six squads of the assault teams had finished scouring the auxiliary buildings. "No survivors," Hank reported. "No sign of any other kids, or of that tall guy with the creepy robes, or the girl he was carrying."

"I don't see how they could get through the lines," the Captain mused. "We've had the entire place surrounded in the first five minutes."

"Must be another way out," Bear said. "A back door, maybe? Through those ruined apartments to the north?"

"Seems unlikely to me," Hank said. "But… something…"

"Tunnel," Rosie said.

"Of course!" Bear said. "Quick! To the boat landing!"

The landing appeared to be deserted. "Let's have a closer look," Bear said to Captain Skeeter, as he climbed out of the commander's hatch. "Rosie, Molly, wait here."

"Wait!" Rosie urged. "We have to stay with—"

It was too late. Bear and Captain Skeeter were already on the ground, running for the boat landing.

Tommy, the leader of the team set to guard the landing, approached and said, "No sign of motion here, Captain. It's been as quiet as a cemetery." His shoulders drooped. "I guess we missed all the fun, eh, Cap?"

"I suppose so," Captain Skeeter said. "Next time, son, next time. You'll get your chance."

Tommy opened his mouth to speak, but his reply was cut off. At the same time, a bloom of bright red blood appeared on his forehead. He looked momentarily surprised, then fell to the ground, dead.

"Get down!" Bear yelled to the fire team. "Skeeter, back to the Bradley!" But it was too late. A score of men piled out of a concealed tunnel entrance. In seconds, the entire fire team was dead. As Bear ran for the tank, he saw Captain Skeeter go down, bleeding profusely from his shoulder. Bear reached for the Bradley, but felt a blow in his thigh, then he, too, was falling. Another blow struck him high in the chest. *Funny how it doesn't really hurt.* He was on the ground, now, fighting desperately to remain conscious. His last thought as the blackness closed in was *I should have stayed with the Bradley. I'm sorry, Rosie Girl…*

— Chapter 21 —

SCUM

B EAR FORCED HIS eyes open, but it was completely dark. His leg was on fire and breathing was difficult. He reached out in the void, but the movement caused a wave of pain to wash over him, and the darkness returned.

* * *

The next time he came to, he kept his eyes closed. He was terribly thirsty. *I'm probably bleeding out.* He extended his right arm tentatively and felt a cold, smooth, hard surface. A vibration rose from beneath him, punctuated by the occasional liquid *slap!* Water on the hull. A boat, he was in a boat! Then, darkness again.

* * *

He woke with a start. The vibration had stopped. A soft orange glow of sunlight penetrated the translucent hull. Bear blinked and looked around. He was lying on a sort of bed, or bunk. There was someone next to him, someone with long, brown hair. Echo?

He felt for a pulse in her throat, but there was none. Whoever it was, she was dead.

He tried to sit up, but the world around him transformed into a Hell of pain. He relaxed, tried to pull his thoughts together: he was on a boat, with a dead girl who might be Echo, and the boat had stopped moving. He heard muffled voices outside the boat, but was unable to make sense of them. And then he was unconscious again.

*　*　*

When he once more regained consciousness, he was lying on a cot in a concrete jail cell with iron bars along the front side. Chains bound his ankles and wrists together. With his right hand, he tentatively explored his chest wound. A bandage covered it, though it was still throbbing. He tried to touch his leg wound, but he couldn't reach it.

He swung his legs over the edge of the cot, onto the floor, then slowly, carefully, he sat up. Oh, man, what a headache! He blinked to clear the crud from his eyes. He was alone in the cell. There was no sign of the dead girl or anyone else, for that matter. He wondered if he was going to lose his leg.

He replayed in his mind the last few moments before he had passed out. It was all a blur, but was slowly coming together. He'd rushed down to the boat landing to intercept the escaping Iron Sceptre, but had been overwhelmed by Fury soldiers. Where had they come from? There must have been a tunnel, as he suspected.

His swirling thoughts and images coalesced a little, and he recalled the militiamen who were guarding the boat being gunned down in a heartbeat. Tommy, the team leader, was dead, but Bear wasn't sure about Captain Skeeter.

And Rosie! What had become of poor little Rosie? He thought hard. The last he remembered, she was still in the gunner's hatch, her hands on the machine gun. Maybe she killed them all and got away! No, that couldn't be right, otherwise he wouldn't be here in this cell.

If only they had waited for the other squads to accompany them! If only he'd stayed with the Bradley! If only. *That is what comes from getting old and careless and forgetting that you are not bullet-proof.*

He thought about the dead girl next to him on the boat ride. Was she really dead? Bear wasn't so sure, now. Was she the same girl who was on the altar during whatever ritual was happening?

Where could that horse's backside in the robe have gone to? Probably lurking around here somewhere. Or not. Bear stood up, with difficulty, putting as little weight as possible on his wounded leg. He limped to the bars and looked up and down the dimly lit corridor. There was a cell across from his own, but it was empty. There was no one in the corridor. He limped back to his cot, lay down again, and waited.

* * *

Clang-clang-clang! Some jerk was pounding on the bars. A phrase came to Bear's mind, a phrase that was popular during the War: cruel and unusual punishment.

"All right, all right, already!" Bear growled. "I'm awake. What do you want?"

"Toilet time." The voice came from a middle-aged soldier in a blue Fury uniform. "Come with me. And don't try anything— boss says if you do, I should go ahead and kill you. Got it?"

"I got it. How about taking these chains off?"

The soldier just laughed. "Go ahead of me down the corridor. The toilet is the last door on the right."

Bear shuffled down the corridor, his leg chains necessitating short little steps. He stopped at the door to the toilet. "You wanna loosen the wrist chains a little? Or would you rather come in and hold it for me?"

The guard made a sour face, but loosened the chains a small amount. He drew his sidearm. "I wouldn't try anything if I were you."

"Don't worry about it." Bear went into the toilet cubicle, took care of his business, washed his hands in a tiny sink, and came out again. "Good to see that The Fury think clean hands are a good idea."

"'Cleanliness is next to Godliness,'" the jailer quipped.

"Cleanliness is next to impossible in a joint like this," Bear said. "But I do appreciate the sink."

"Back to your cell," the jailer said. "You're about to have visitors. Or a visitor, at least."

"Better spruce up, then," Bear said. He ran his still-wet fingers through his bushy hair and beard. "Gotta look good for visitors."

The jailer tightened Bear's chains, then locked him up again. "You just wait right there, old fellow. Someone will be along in due course."

"Great plan," Bear said. "Wait right here, I mean. I guess I'll just do that."

The jailer grinned. "I guess you will." He shambled off down the corridor.

Bear waited. And waited, and waited.

At last, there came the sound of a distant door opening, followed by footsteps, and, in his own sweet time, the jailer appeared. He looked tired. "Okay, old-timer, on your feet." He opened the cell door while Bear struggled to rise. "You're not going to give me any trouble, are you, old fellow? I'm just not in the mood for trouble today. Had plenty of trouble already, what with people coming and going, getting cells ready, getting them food and water and walking them to the john." He sighed. "Get a move on—it's been a long day."

Bear shuffled out of the cell as rapidly as the leg chains permitted. The jailer led him all the way down the corridor, past the toilet, to a very solid-looking metal door. The jailer knocked three times, then called out, "Prisoner coming through. Open up."

The door opened, and the jailer handed Bear over to a uniformed escort of four Fury soldiers. "So long, old-timer. It's been nice knowing you, more or less. I don't expect we'll see each other again."

Bear didn't care for the sound of that, but before he could ask any questions, the apparent leader of the escort punched him in the belly, doubling him over. "Come on, *scum*. Let's move."

Scum, is it? I guess we'll see about that. His leg was on fire and his chest wound had started bleeding again. One of the soldiers jerked his chain savagely, nearly causing Bear to topple over, but Bear caught himself and half-limped, half-shuffled as fast as he could manage.

The soldiers led him down a maze of passages, all alike: brick floor, metal walls, and a metal ceiling punctuated by dim electric lights providing barely enough light to walk safely.

Bear's distorted time sense prevented him from guessing how far they walked. It seemed like hours, but it wasn't likely that there was a tunnel or a building that big. Eventually, they arrived at another metal door, much like the first one. "Prisoner escort," the lead soldier said, and the door opened to admit them to a room blazing with light.

Bear blinked and squinted against the harsh, actinic glare. He raised his hand to shield his eyes but was prevented by his chains, so he ducked his head as far down as he could. As his sight returned, he could see that he was at the edge of an enormous hall. An altar stood on a platform at one end, similar to the altar at the temple.

On the altar stood the same tall man he'd seen at the temple earlier, wearing the same dark hooded robe. In the harsh light, Bear could discern mysterious symbols embroidered into the fabric. A low table stood on each side of the man. A female figure lay on each table, covered with a cloth that had the same symbols as the robe. Their faces were covered, so Bear couldn't tell if they were his girls, but one was blond, and the other brunette, so he allowed himself a small measure of hope.

The tall man turned slowly to face Bear. He pulled back his hood to reveal a long, thin, ascetic face covered in part by a full beard that tapered down to the middle of his chest. He slowly extended his arms as though he were blessing the crowds. In a voice that rumbled like mountain thunder, he intoned, "Man-called-Bear, Bear-called-Man, come join your daughters."

— Chapter 22 —

THE IRON SCEPTRE

BEAR GROWLED, "IF you've laid a single finger on those girls—"

The escort leader slammed the butt of his rifle into Bear's kidney. Bear dropped to his hands and knees and vomited onto the shiny wooden floor.

"You'll what?" the tall man mocked. "You won't do anything at all, you lowlife scum, except everything I tell you. You're nothing, understand? Nothing!" He filled the auditorium with his insane, maniacal laughter. "I am the Iron Sceptre!" he declared, to no one or everyone. "The *Iron Sceptre*, do you hear? I, and I alone, say what happens here."

Bear took a long, sideways look at the man. *He's certifiable, a complete whack job—and he has my girls.*

"All right, then, Mr. Iron Sceptre, you're the boss," Bear said soothingly. "Now that you've got me, how about letting my girls go?"

"Oh, I wouldn't think of it, Mr. Bear-man. These girls have an extraordinary destiny ahead of them."

"And what might that be?" Bear asked. *As if I couldn't guess.*

"They are to become my queens, the bearers of my seed to times indefinite!"

"And how are you going to manage that, exactly?" Bear asked.

"How do you think, Bear-man? I shall impregnate them in a sacred ceremony, right here in this holy tabernacle, and you shall bear witness." He giggled a little, and his voice lost its majestic, sonorous tones. "The Bear Man will Bear Witness! He'll be a Witness Bearer Bear. A Witness Bear." He giggled again. "How do you like that idea, eh, Mr. Witness-Bearer-Bear Man?" The thunderous voice was back. "Now, get to your feet and come unto me!"

Bear struggled to his feet. His wounded leg wasn't going to take much more abuse before it gave out altogether.

The escort leader jabbed him in the small of his back with the barrel of his rifle and snarled, "Move it. You heard his Holiness."

Bear shuffled forward toward the raised platform. Anything that got him closer to the girls was fine with him. He turned his head and spoke to the escort leader. "His Holiness, is it? You don't really swallow that malarkey, do you? He's no holy man—he's a raving lunatic."

"Shut your mouth," the escort leader hissed. "I don't care what he is, as long as I get my turn with the girls when he's done."

"Oh, so that's how it works. He rapes them, then you get a turn. And I suppose your mates, here, get their turn after you?"

"Shut up, I said. I told you before." He gave Bear another jab with the rifle.

"A word of advice, sonny. You stick me with that rifle barrel again, and I'm going to bust out of these chains, take that gun away from you, and break it over your head. Just sayin.'"

One of the girls spoke from under her cover. "You'd better listen to him," she said faintly. "He's not a tame bear."

Was that Rosie? Was she still alive after all?

The escort leader drew his rifle back for another poke at Bear, then changed his mind. "Just keep moving," the young soldier said. "Anyway, you'll do nothing of the kind, because we'll be feasting on your fat, greasy corpse."

"I've heard rumors about cannibalism among The Fury," Bear said quietly. "Thank you for confirming it. Now I'll feel a lot easier."

"Easier?"

"Less guilty."

"Less guilty for what?"

"For wiping your entire sick, pathetic, demented little cult off the face of the Earth for all time." Bear grinned a great savage grin at the escort leader, who involuntarily took a step backward. "That prancing maniac won't be able to save you. There's just no place in Bear's world for little-girl-raping cannibals."

"Shut UP!" the escort leader screamed and jabbed Bear with the rifle barrel again.

In one fluid motion, Bear whipped around, yanked the rifle out of the escort leader's hands, and, holding it by the barrel, dashed the escort leader's brains out of his skull onto the floor.

Rosie shook her head sadly. "I told you."

The other three Fury soldiers commenced beating Bear about the head and body with their rifles.

Bear's chains prevented him from covering his head, so he dived for the floor and curled into as small a ball as his bulk permitted.

"Stop that! Stop that at once!" came the deep voice from the altar. "I told you I want him *alive* for the ceremony. Find someone to clean up that mess. He's spilled his brains all over my clean floor. How can I have a holy ceremony with brains on the floor? Huh? How? Tell me that!" He was screaming now. "Cart that mess out and dump it in the river. All that idiot had to do was keep his mouth shut like I told him. Oh, and Bobby is the escort leader now. You think you can get that Bear-man over here, Bobby? Fine. Go get more help if you think you need it."

"Yes, Holiness," Bobby said. "I think we can manage. He's nearly unconscious now, anyway." Bobby and his minions tried to get Bear to his feet, but Bear was too woozy to stand on his own. They tried dragging him, first by his hair, then by his boots. Finally, Bobby sent one minion for more soldiers.

No one spoke while they waited for help to arrive. Shortly, another squad of eight soldiers returned with Bobby's minion, and the eleven of them half-walked, half-carried Bear onto the platform, where the Iron Sceptre awaited them wearing a bored expression. "Just prop him up in that big red chair," the Iron Sceptre pronounced. "Fasten his chains to the chair. Position the chair between the sacrificial tables—we want our guest of honor to have a good view of the ceremony, don't we? Bobby, you and your men stay here and see that the bear-man doesn't get loose, somehow. Do you think you can do that?"

"Yes, your Holiness."

"Well, that's just fine. The rest of you go fetch our other guests and seat them in the audience. The first row, mind you—I want them to have the best possible view of the ceremony."

Bear watched through bruised and bleeding eyes as the eight soldiers left the great hall. He held onto the chair with one hand in an effort to keep the room from spinning, but with small success. He kept fading in and out of consciousness and was finding it hard to follow what was happening on the altar. The Iron Sceptre was fussing with various gleaming, unpleasant-looking shiny metal instruments laid out on a long side table with a white tablecloth. He was speaking in a kind of murmuring chant that was unintelligible to Bear.

The eight soldiers returned with even more soldiers escorting a handful of Johnsonite militiamen. Three of them, it looked like, or was it four? Bear peered through his curtain of blood. He couldn't tell for sure. The Fury soldiers set the new prisoners one by one in the front-row seats directly in front of the altar.

Bear thought he recognized the first one—it was Tommy, Tommy the squad leader! But how could that be? He'd seen Tommy shot through the head. He squinted against the glare. Yes, it was Tommy, and he was quite dead—Bear could see the bullet hole in his forehead, its ragged edges still oozing a little.

The Fury soldiers seated the second prisoner right next to Tommy. He was easy to recognize: it was Captain Skeeter. Was he dead, too? No, he was moaning and trying to move his head. One of the Fury was slapping his face and telling him to wake up, while another ensured that he was securely chained to the theater seat.

Bear wondered how Captain Skeeter could be here, because he'd been killed at the boat landing. Hadn't he? No, Bear remembered with some difficulty, but he was shot in the shoulder. We should have stayed in the Bradley, he told himself for the thousandth time. If only… well, too late for that now. He was moaning, so he probably was still alive, but in what condition? Bear couldn't tell.

A few minutes later, several dozen Fury soldiers entered the auditorium, spread out into little groups, and took their seats. They were in a festive mood, laughing and joking. Bear could hear snatches of the conversation. It seemed to be mostly concerned with the activities scheduled for after the imminent ceremony, including who was going to be allotted which corpse for specific sexual purposes before the corpses were prepared for the evening meal.

Bear resisted the urge to vomit again. He needed to keep his head, to focus on what was going on around him. The Iron Sceptre had turned his attention to the females on the tables on each side of Bear's chair. He approached the table on Bear's right and drew the white silk covering down to the girl's chest, exposing her face. Echo! It was Echo! But was she dead or alive?

"Behold, oh mighty Bear-man! Your daughter, the brown-haired one. She was beside you on the boat, though I doubt you remember. What a beauty she is! So young, so tender, so pure." The Iron Sceptre bent and caressed her cheek, then stood again.

But as he caressed her, Bear saw her eyelids flutter. She was alive! Then Bear's heart sank in his chest. He wasn't sure if she might be better off dead.

Next, the Iron Sceptre turned to the supine figure on Bear's left. He pulled down the silk covering, the same as he had Echo's.

Rosie! It was Rosie! She was alive, too! But Bear already knew that—she'd spoken, hadn't she?

"This one is already with child," the Iron Sceptre informed his audience. He ran his hand over Rosie's incipient baby bump. "That presents a minor problem as far as her bearing my seed is concerned. So tonight's ceremony will be merely symbolic in her case. Later, we will remove the impediment and impregnate her the same as the other."

He returned to the podium. "Now the time has come to begin our Most Holy Ceremony. Bobby, if you'll be so kind as to cut Mr. Bear-man's clothes away, we can get started."

— Chapter 23 —

ONLY MOSTLY DEAD

Bobby hesitantly began cutting Bear's enormous fur coat off the huge man. It was real fur, made of real bear skin, and Bobby had a tough time trying to get through it with his less-than-razor-sharp combat knife, which amused Bear to the point of chuckling.

The chuckling, in turn, enraged the Iron Sceptre, who snatched a rifle from one of Bobby's subordinates, and clubbed Bear over the head with it. It was a most ineffectual clubbing, which further amused Bear, and that further enraged the Iron Sceptre.

Little by little, Bear's fur coat came away in small, ragged patches, revealing his red woolen one-piece long-johns underneath. The long-johns caused Rosie to smile a little, which the Iron Sceptre wiped off her face with a savage backhand blow.

Bear growled when the Iron Sceptre slapped Rosie, which earned him another blow with the rifle. Bear could feel his skull bones starting to crack. His vision was blurred; he was dizzy and nauseated. He was pretty sure that he had multiple concussions.

Bobby kept sawing away at Bear's clothing. The woolen long johns didn't take nearly as much cutting as the fur coat. Bear was so hairy that, when he was completely naked, he didn't look all that different from when he was wearing his fur coat.

The Iron Sceptre towered over Bear. "Well, look at you, naked as a jaybird. What a sight to see!"

Bear wondered exactly how naked a jaybird was, but decided not to ask. The Iron Sceptre's pupils were dilated, his eyes were wide and crazy-looking, and he was quivering all over. Bear decided to keep still for the moment. Almost certainly the Sceptre was strung out on some kind of psychoactive drug. *Well, of course.*

The Iron Sceptre assumed his sonorous voice and decreed, "As our guest of honor, I generously grant you the privilege of First Seed. You and the blond one—Rosie, you call her?—seem to know each other. I command you now, in the name of the Loward, to plant your seed in the young maiden."

The soldiers hauled Bear to his feet and kept him from falling. They maneuvered him to Rosie's side. The Iron Sceptre whisked the sheet off Rosie, revealing her naked body. *She's still so thin I can count her ribs. Didn't have time to feed her enough cheeseburgers.* Out loud, he addressed the Iron Sceptre, "Not a chance, you degenerate pervert. What a disgusting idea. Anyway, as you can see, she's pregnant already, so what's the point?"

"The point," the Iron Sceptre roared, "is that you"—he made a sweeping gesture encompassing the entire audience—"all of you, must obey me in all things. I am the Iron Sceptre, anointed by the Loward himself, your leader and ruler in every way. Now, Bearman, obey me. Proceed with the ceremony."

Bear murmured something too low to hear.

"What's that? What did you say?" The Iron Sceptre was raging now.

"You heard me," Bear growled. "And the horse you rode in on, too."

The Iron Sceptre flushed purple and gave a signal, at which Bobby and his minions started giving Bear the most savage beating of his life. They used fists, boots, and rifle butts. By the time they were done, Bear lay in a heap on the floor, nearly unconscious.

The Iron Sceptre signaled, a mere flick of his fingers, and the beating stopped. Bear groaned and tried to roll over, but he was not able. Bobby and his minions hauled Bear to his feet again, but this time they had to support Bear's limp body to keep him from crashing back to the ground.

"One more chance," the Iron Sceptre said, in a cajoling tone. "All you have to do is plant your seed in the young virgin—oh, yes, we checked—and complete the Fertility Ceremony. Then you can rest and have your wounds tended to."

Rosie shouted at the Iron Sceptre, "You think I care? Bear and I are married, anyway. Have been for quite a while. Whose baby do you *think* I'm carrying? I don't care what your filthy virginity check told you—I doubt you've ever seen a woman before!" Then, in a whisper, "It's okay, Mr. The Bear. Really, I don't mind. Just get it done, then we can both rest." She squeezed her eyes shut, and steeled herself for the ritual.

"Not going to happen," Bear grunted. "Not now, not ever. I'll die first." He wriggled loose and collapsed to the floor.

"That you will!" the Iron Sceptre intoned. "Go ahead, Bobby, beat him to death! *Now!*"

Bobby and his two companions proceeded to do exactly that. They beat Bear unconscious, then beat him beyond recognition, then beat him until the blood ran from his nose and ears. At the end, Bear was no longer reacting to the blows, not even twitching as they rained down upon him.

At last, the Iron Sceptre commanded Bobby to stop. "He's done for. No one could survive such an ordeal. Still, he must be admired for holding out as long as he has." He turned and pulled the silk covering from Echo. "We will start with this one, then. She's no virgin, anyway. Bobby, you may have the honor as a reward for your excellent service today."

Bobby dropped his pants and hunched over Echo's bare body. Echo never so much as twitched; she remained completely inert, motionless.

Rosie, tears streaming, couldn't bring herself to watch Bobby and Echo. Instead, she wept for Bear, lying in a heap beside her, motionless. "Oh, Bear," she said, over and over. "I'm so sorry. I *told* you it was okay. Why didn't you save yourself?" She glanced at the Iron Sceptre, who was watching Bobby intently. He was entranced, his eyes glazed over, a strange expression on his face. Rosie reached out and caressed Bear's broken cheek.

As she did so, she thought she saw Bear's eyelids flicker. She caressed him again. Yes, his eyelids were fluttering. He opened his eyes and looked at Rosie.

Rosie was about to speak, but Bear shook his head the tiniest little bit. "We showed him, didn't we, Rosie Girl?" Bear's voice was the barest whisper. "I'm sorry I can't get you out of here. I'm all out of options."

Rosie leaned toward him and dropped a small bit of twisted wire near Bear's face. She whispered, "It's one of the clips holding the sheet down. When the tall man pulled the sheet off me, I grabbed it."

Bear slowly reached up with one chained hand, took the clip, and examined it. "I don't know. But it's a thousand times better than what we had a moment ago. Uh-oh, it looks like Bobby is getting finished over there. Go back to 'sleep.'"

Rosie closed her eyes again. Bear forced himself to become completely limp, only his hand moved slowly beneath his body.

Bobby finished his disgusting business and pulled up his trousers. One of his soldiers began unfastening his uniform pants. "My turn next, right?"

"Not so fast!" the Iron Sceptre snapped. "Keep your pants on. I, myself, shall proceed with the next part of the ceremony. Behold as I plant my Holy Seed into the maiden." He positioned himself at the foot of Rosie's table, then with one swift movement removed his hood and robe, revealing himself in all his naked, hairless glory, in an obvious state of readiness. The previous 'ceremony' with Echo appeared to have heightened his state of arousal. He loomed over Rosie's emaciated body. "Spread your knees, girl. Don't make this harder than it needs to be."

Rosie crossed her legs at the ankles. Bear emitted a soft chuckle at that, but His Holiness was too distracted to notice. "Submit, girl! Don't be difficult. I promise I'll be gentle."

Rosie squeezed her skinny legs together even harder. The Iron Sceptre fell upon her, trying to pry her legs apart. Bobby and his two minions ran over and helped to pull her knees away to each side.

The Iron Sceptre was poised to consummate the ceremony, but suddenly froze. A deep, angry, growl was coming from somewhere in the room—he couldn't tell exactly where. "What is that? What's that noise?" He backed away from Rosie, looking around in all directions. The growling noise was getting louder and louder. "Where is that coming from?" the Iron Sceptre screamed. "Find it and make it stop!"

Throughout the auditorium, the various soldiers of the audience were searching under the seats and in the aisles, to no avail. Suddenly, one soldier pointed and yelled, "There! Behind you! On the platform!"

The Iron Sceptre whipped around and found himself face to face with the naked Bear, apparently risen from the dead, and much larger than he had seemed earlier. Bear grabbed the Iron Sceptre by his long beard and roared into his face, "WE DO NOT TREAT LITTLE GIRLS THAT WAY! DO YOU HEAR ME? WE DO NOT TREAT ANYONE THAT WAY, NOT EVER, NOT IN MY WORLD!" With that, Bear shook the Iron Sceptre until his eyes rolled around in his ugly head. "NOW FLY! BEGONE WITH YOU!"

Bear picked up the lanky Sceptre, one hand on his neck, one on his hip, lifted him high above his head, and flung him off the stage into a group of soldiers in the third row of the audience. The crack of his spine against the wooden chair backs echoed throughout the auditorium.

Bear wrenched Bobby's rifle from his grip and smashed Bobby's head with the butt, then flipped it around and shot Bobby's two minions. He turned to Rosie, "Help Echo, if you can." Then he forced his wounded body down the steps into the audience, firing as he went.

Rosie covered the unconscious Echo, then, still naked, picked up one of the shiny scalpels from the side table and launched herself among the startled Fury soldiers in the front row, slashing wildly, blood flying everywhere.

Captain Skeeter suddenly looked much less dead than he had previously. With a mighty heave, he broke his chains loose from the flimsy wooden chairs. He spun around, grabbed a soldier, and used him as a shield while he took the soldier's sidearm. He joined Bear in shooting down every last Fury soldier still standing.

Bear limped over to where the Iron Sceptre lay crumpled between two rows of seats.

"Is he still alive?" Captain Skeeter called out.

Bear felt for a pulse. At his touch, the Iron Sceptre blinked twice, groaned, and begged hoarsely, "Help me. I can't feel my feet. Help me, please."

Bear shrugged and shot him three times in the face. "I'm afraid he's dead, Captain," Bear said. And they both grinned, for the first time in a long while.

— Chapter 24 —

Horatius at the Bridge

Rosie, still holding the scalpel and dripping with blood, came over and took a long look at the former head of the Loward's Fury. "Is he dead?" she asked quietly.

Bear said gently, "Yes, Rosie Girl, he's dead."

"Good!" Rosie said. "Let's make sure the rest of them are dead, too!" And she took her scalpel and made the rounds of the fallen Fury soldiers. When she was sure that every one of them was all the way dead, she went to look after Echo.

Echo was still unconscious, but shivering. Rosie tucked the silk covering around her, then made a makeshift sarong for herself out of the other.

Next, she stripped a couple of uniforms from the dead Fury soldiers, and put one on. Bear and Captain Skeeter helped her dress Echo in the other.

"She's still out," Bear said. He sniffed at her lips, then opened an eyelid and checked her pupils. "I think she's been drugged."

"Just as well," Captain Skeeter said. "If she's fortunate, she won't remember much of anything."

"I hope not, for her sake," Bear said.

Clothes for Bear was another problem: his fur coat was in shreds on the stage, and there wasn't a Fury soldier more than half his size. Bear collected a few items from the dead soldiers, then hooked two web belts together to make one long one, which he strapped around his waist, to which he began attaching weapons and other accoutrements. In the interest of modesty, he tried tucking some of the larger scraps of his fur coat into the belt, but they all fell out before he had taken three steps.

Rosie giggled at that, which made Bear frown and blush—all over—which made Captain Skeeter laugh out loud. Bear started to growl again, but Rosie said, "It's kinda late to be worried about your modesty, now. I mean, after all, we were almost married, right?"

Bear blushed even harder, and said, "Look, Rosie Girl, let's not even talk about that, okay?"

"I'm not body-shy," Rosie said. "I told you that before. So why should you be?"

"Because I'm old-fashioned," Bear roared. "Change the subject!"

"One thing, though," Captain Skeeter said with a twinkle in his eye. "You'd better not let any of those Fury soldiers see you like that."

Bear narrowed his eyes and glared at the Captain. "Is that so? And why might that be, pray tell?"

"Well, most of them are pretty young, you see. And if they were to see *that*"—he pointed—"well, they'd never feel like men again in their lives."

"Doggone it!" Bear said. "I can't help the way I'm—"

But it was too late. Rosie and Captain Skeeter were belly-laughing. They laughed until the tears ran down. It was contagious laughter, and Bear finally had to join them.

"Okay," Bear said. "We'll just have to live with it, for now. Maybe we'll find something my size later. Besides, the shock value might be helpful."

"That's about the *size* of it," Captain Skeeter said nonchalantly.

Rosie cracked up again, which started another round of laughter.

But when it had died down, Bear sat down heavily in the front row near Echo and held his head in both hands. "Don't make me laugh any more—it hurts."

Rosie ran to him. "What is it, Mr. The Bear? Are you okay?"

"I don't feel so good all of a sudden."

"Blood loss, maybe," Captain Skeeter said. "The adrenaline is wearing off. You might be going into shock."

Bear didn't answer. His skin had turned gray and pallid.

"What's shock?" Rosie asked.

"It happens when there's not enough blood in the body," Captain Skeeter said. "Look at his bandages. The one on his side is soaked through, and the one on his leg looks pretty bad, too. He's lost a lot of blood, I'll bet. And we don't even know what happened on his way here." He handed a canteen to Bear.

Bear removed the lid, sniffed the contents, and took a long pull, then smacked his lips. "Is whiskey good for treating shock?"

Captain Skeeter snatched the canteen away from Bear. He was about to pour it out, then thought better of it. He took a long drink of the whiskey, then handed the canteen back to Bear. "Beats me," he said. "Can't see that it'll hurt much, in your condition. Or maybe I have that backward."

"Too late," Bear said. "We'll just have to use the Empirical Method to find out." He handed the empty canteen back to the Captain. "Here, take this, see if you can find some actual water."

"I have water." Rosie put her canteen to Bear's lips. He was only half conscious, now, but he sipped what remained. Together, Rosie and the Captain laid Bear down. Captain Skeeter gathered as much clothing as he could find and made makeshift blankets to cover Bear. They rolled up some of the extra uniforms to use to elevate his feet.

Captain Skeeter took the canteen from Rosie. "I'm going to find some more water."

"I think I'll just stay here and sleep a little," Bear mumbled.

"Better not," Captain Skeeter said. "Fatigue is a sign of shock, too. Try to stay awake until I get back, okay?"

"Sure thing," Bear said, as he drifted off to sleep.

"That's not good. Watch him, Rosie," Captain Skeeter said. "If his breathing changes, call me, then try to wake him up. And make sure he stays warm."

"Okay."

"I won't be long. There's likely a kitchen or a restroom or a drinking fountain or *something* around here. I have to be careful, which will slow me down a bit. We have no idea if there are more soldiers in this place. Rosie, you stay on guard in case someone comes in." He disappeared through the nearest door into the corridor.

Rosie felt Bear's forehead, though she wasn't really sure why. It was cold and clammy. She moved some of the makeshift blankets aside and snuggled up as close as she could to Bear. "Don't die, Mr. The Bear," she whispered. "Try to hold on. I'm not done with you yet."

Captain Skeeter returned with several filled canteens. Between the two of them, the Captain and Rosie got Bear to drink almost two liters of water. Bear got a little of his color back but was still very sleepy.

"Rosie," Captain Skeeter said quietly, "we're definitely not alone here. When I was getting the water, I heard noises from somewhere in the building. They sounded like they were far off, but it was really hard to be certain. Can you watch Bear again while I gather some weapons?"

Rosie nodded.

"There are only a few weapons in this auditorium. We already have that Bobby person's rifle, and those of his two men. We have quite a few sidearms that belonged to the Fury soldiers in the audience. I didn't see any more weapons when I got the water. But there must be an arsenal somewhere in the building, right?"

"I don't want you to leave us here again," Rosie said. "I'd feel a lot better if we all went together."

"I understand," the Captain said, "but that's really not possible. I can move around reasonably well, but Bear is unconscious and can't walk. We'd better plan to make our stand right here. The only ammunition we have is in these three rifles and the pistols. No spare clips that I could find. These soldiers were attending a ceremony, not a military function. So I need to find us some more firepower."

Bear struggled up onto one elbow. "I'm feeling a bit better now. I might be able to walk a little." He tried to get to his feet but was too weak. He settled back down to the floor. "On the other hand, maybe not so much."

"Glad you're conscious again," Captain Skeeter said. "That's a good sign. Still thirsty?" He handed Bear the last full canteen. "We don't have unlimited choices," he continued. "We can make our stand here until our ammo is gone. I can go scout for more ammo and weapons. Or we can try to find our way out before someone finds us. What do you think?"

"Beats me," Bear said groggily.

"Do you have any idea where we are?" Captain Skeeter asked Bear.

Bear considered. "No. Well, maybe. Somewhere near the river. I woke up on a boat, no idea how long I'd been on it. You?"

"They brought me overland. Took forever. I had a sack over my head, plus I was inside a closed wagon."

"Horse-drawn? Electric? Gasoline? Might help us judge distance."

"Gasoline, I guess. It felt like we were going pretty fast."

Bear sagged. "Going pretty fast for a long time. That's a lot of territory."

"Maybe we could make our way outside, get a look around?"

"Maybe," Bear said. "I'm not going to go very far with this leg wound." Then he indicated his bandaged chest. "And I don't know how bad this is, but it can't be good. And I'm pretty sure my head bones are broken, some of them, anyway."

"Maybe we can find a vehicle."

"Maybe *you* can find a vehicle. I'm going to sit right here, I think. Leave me one of the rifles, take Rosie out through the tunnel where I came in. I'll make my last stand here, try to buy you some time."

"Horatius at the bridge, eh? Well, it's a thought. Wouldn't be my first choice."

"Mine neither," Bear said, "but it might be our only chance."

"Who's Horatius?" Rosie asked.

"Old Roman soldier," Bear said. "Held off an entire invading army all by himself by defending one end of a bridge. Gave his army time to cross the bridge, then destroy it."

"Destroy it?" Rosie said. "But didn't that leave the Horatius dude on the—oh. Oh, *no*! Oh, please, not that." She threw her arms around Bear's ample waist and hugged him tightly. "I won't let you!"

Bear hugged her back. "I don't think we're going to have much choice, Rosie Girl. I hear some kind of commotion starting in the corridor. Sounds like a whole lot of people coming our way, and coming fast."

A lot of shouting punctuated by the reports of small-arms fire sounded in the distance, drawing steadily closer. As the sound of the crowd grew louder, however, the small-arms fire became less frequent.

Captain Skeeter handed a rifle each to Bear and Rosie, then directed them to move close to the rear exit door, where Bear had come in.

Rosie helped Bear into position, then turned, kneeled, and rested the barrel of her own rifle on the back of the seat alongside the Captain.

"Remember what I taught you," Bear said. "Hit them in the body and keep shooting until they stop moving."

"I remember, Mr. The Bear."

"Better set it to three-round bursts," the Captain said. "Conserve ammunition. When it's gone, we're done. Safety off."

The commotion in the corridor had reached the doors of the auditorium. There came a brief hush, then all of the doors crashed open at once to admit an entire army.

The Bear and The Rose

— Chapter 25 —

HANK

"**H**OLD YOUR FIRE until we know for sure who it is," Bear whispered. "It's a lot harder to un-kill someone you wish was still alive. Believe me, I know."

The incoming troops must have had the same idea because they stopped just inside the doorway. After a moment of tense silence, a voice from the new crowd called out, "Who's in there?"

At the same instant, Captain Skeeter shouted, "Halt and identify yourself!"

After another brief silence, the same voice called again from the doorway, "Cap? Is that you? It's me, Hank!"

Captain Skeeter and Bear exchanged a doubtful look, then the Captain instructed, "Drop your weapon and advance, slowly, down the aisle."

Hank did so, slowly, hands raised above his head. When it was clear that the newcomer was, indeed, Hank, Captain Skeeter stood up slowly and identified himself.

Hank looked around the room and whistled softly. "What happened here, Cap?"

"Bear happened, that's what."

"Hank," Bear said from his kneeling position. "Good to see you, son. Forgive me for not getting up. I'm slightly out of commission at the moment."

Hank looked Bear over. "Uhh… good to *see* you, too, Bear. Though I never really expected to see that much of you all at once." He smiled broadly.

"I seem to have misplaced my coat," Bear said.

"Also his underwear," Rosie chipped in.

Bear scowled and shot Rosie a look, but said nothing.

"You have a medical team?" Captain Skeeter asked. "Bear is pretty badly banged up, and the girl on the floor over there has been unconscious for a while."

"Corporal Hanshaw!" Hank called. "Get the medics down here at once."

"Yes, sir!"

"And, Corporal," Captain Skeeter said, "pass the word up the line that some of our people are wearing Fury uniforms."

"'Some of us' is right," Rosie said under her breath and giggled again. "Others not so much."

"Hush, now, Rosie Girl," Bear said, but he was smiling.

Captain Skeeter was smiling, too. "Hanshaw, send one of your guys to find a painting tarp or a boat cover and bring it down here. Anything big will do. Infield cover, maybe—check the ball field."

Bear growled, "Stop, already. Infield cover, indeed."

The medical team arrived. One pair of medics examined Echo, then put her on a stretcher.

"Easy with her," Bear said. "She's been through a lot today."

"Will do," one of the medics said. They carried her down the aisle and out of the room.

"How about you?" a med-tech asked Rosie.

"Oh, I'm fine. Just tired."

Captain Skeeter said, "She'll need a full checkup back at the base. I think she'll be okay for now. She needs to be hydrated and fed."

"Yes, sir," said the med-tech. "Tell you what—how about you hop up on the stretcher, here, young lady, and we'll give you a free ride to the ambulance."

"I won't leave Bear," Rosie said.

The med-tech looked inquiringly at Captain Skeeter, who nodded an okay.

Meanwhile, three teams were working on Bear: one on his leg, another on his chest wound, and the third was examining his concussions. One medic rigged up an IV, while another gave Bear a series of injections.

"What's all that?" Rosie asked.

"The IV is to keep him hydrated, to prevent shock. It has glucose in it, a kind of sugar the body needs. He's right on the edge of shock now."

"He was in shock earlier," Captain Skeeter said, "but he rallied for a bit."

"That's not necessarily a good thing," the medical technician said. "He's going to need a lot of rest and hydration. The injections are to help his body function until he can do it on his own again."

Rosie nodded, frowning.

"Don't worry, Miss," the technician said. "I think we got here in time. We're getting his wounds patched up, and the bleeding stopped." He watched the other team work on Bear's leg. "How's it going?"

"It's going okay," one of the leg medics said. "We might even save the leg."

"You've gotta save the leg," Rosie said. "He wouldn't be The Bear without it!"

"He's your father, Miss?"

"Yes. Yes, he is."

"Well, don't worry, we're doing the best we can." Then to the Captain, "I think he's about ready to move now. We, uh, we might need some extra guys. And, umm, we could use something to cover him up. Our blankets aren't really doing the job."

A militiaman stepped forward carrying a pair of king-sized quilted bedspreads.

The chief medic brightened. "That'll do just fine," he said.

The medics wrapped Bear in the bedspreads and got him onto the stretcher. Bear was fading in and out of consciousness, but seemed to appreciate the blankets.

"We'll have you warmed up in no time," the chief medic told him. "Okay, men, let's try it with six of you." They took up positions around the stretcher. "On three: one, two, three!"

The other team—only two men—picked up Rosie's stretcher, and she followed Bear to the medical wagon.

"We'll see you at the base hospital in just a little while," Captain Skeeter said. Then, to Hank, "Let's head back to the convoy, shall we?"

"Nothing doing, Cap," Hank said emphatically. "You're going with the rest of the wounded in the medical wagon."

"But—"

"No 'buts', Cap. I'm in charge now, and that's how it has to be."

Captain Skeeter subsided. "You know, Hank, I have to tell you: I've never been so glad to see anyone in my life as I was to see you. How in the world did you find us?"

"Well, Cap, it wasn't easy, until it was."

"How so?"

"Back at the temple, you know, you guys and the Bradley disappeared so fast that it took the rest of us a moment to catch up." He looked at Captain Skeeter reproachfully. "You should have stayed with the vehicle like you said, you know."

"I know. You're absolutely right."

"Well, when we realized you were gone, we got a couple of squads together and followed you to the landing. We heard some shots, but when we got there the boat and everyone were gone. Couldn't see much of it as it went down the river, and we didn't dare shoot at what we couldn't see."

"Quite right. How did you find this place?"

"At first, we didn't know what to do. You guys were just… *gone.* So we went back to that temple and searched all the rooms again, just to be sure there were no survivors. I gotta tell you, Cap— some of the things we found in those rooms, well, if I'd been sorry we killed them all before, I'd have stopped being sorry after we found all that stuff."

"What kind of stuff?"

"Lots of sex stuff," Hank said, "but the nasty, hurty kind. And… and… well, I hate to say it, but there was some evidence of cannibalism."

"I believe you," Captain Skeeter said. "We saw some of that here, too. Evil bunch of people."

"Not anymore," Hank said. "Anyway, we found this one Fury soldier, couldn't have been more than fifteen, hiding in a supply closet in the basement. We dragged him upstairs and showed him some of the stuff we'd found, and he sang like a canary. He didn't really know too much about the Iron Sceptre and all his rituals, but he had some ideas about where the main tabernacle was."

"How's that?"

"Well, you know, the Loward's Fury started off as part of the Loward's Own, right? This here tabernacle is a relatively short shot back to Diablo, where the Loward's Own started, almost due east. Apparently, the Iron Sceptre broke from the Loward's Own, then migrated west, almost to the airport. Then he turned southward, so he could attack Johnson and our bunch from the north. After that it was pretty easy to figure out the general direction. So we loaded up all the militiamen we could fit into our powered vehicles—those trucks we got this morning were a real help—and went north up the old freeway, as far as we could. We spotted movement and some smoke around the old arena complex, investigated, and found this place. There were Fury soldiers outside, smoking and joking and milling around. Poor discipline, Cap. That's what led to their downfall."

"You got all that from one scared kid?"

"Well, Cap, it took us a while, but he wasn't all that scared. He was certain that the Iron Sceptre himself was on the way to rescue him. He seemed a lot more disappointed than scared. He missed his turn with the girls, you see."

"I see. So where is he now?"

"We shot him and burned his body with the rest of that temple. What did you expect me to do, kiss him?"

— Chapter 26 —

Chubby's Chinese Kitchen

Several days after the Battle of the Tabernacle, as people were beginning to call it, Bear and Rosie walked into the old Chinese restaurant on the corner of the Embarcadero and Third Street. Hank had told them that this was where they would find Johnson himself. They blinked until their eyes were accustomed to the cool, dark interior. The enticing aroma of spicy Chinese cooking wafted from the kitchen. Antique iron latticework decorated the windows and cast long, interesting shadows on the old, worn wooden floor.

In what had once been a large corner booth, a middle-aged man worked amidst a stack of papers scattered over the table. He waved at Bear and Rosie. "Come, come, welcome! Please, join me. I'm so happy to meet you both! I had hoped to meet you at the Militia Headquarters, but as you can see"—he made a broad gesture indicating the scattered papers—"I'm a bit snowed under."

"I would have come sooner, but the nurses in that hospital wouldn't let me go. What exactly is it you do here, Mr. Johnson?" Bear asked. "That is, if you don't mind me asking."

"Just 'Johnson' is fine. I don't mind at all," Johnson replied. "You, both of you, are welcome to ask me anything at all. I have no secrets. What do I do here? I ask myself the same question. I help out with all sorts of things, getting them organized. Mostly, I move paper from one stack to another. Please, won't you sit down? Can I get you something to eat or drink?"

"Well," Bear said, "now that mention it, whatever's cooking in the kitchen smells pretty good. I wouldn't say no to a little snack." He and Rosie slid into the booth together, opposite Johnson, while Molly made herself comfortable on the floor beneath the table.

"Chubby!" Johnson called to a rotund chef, apparently of Asian descent. "Would you please bring some snacks and tea for our guests?"

"Sure thing, Boss," came a voice from the kitchen.

Johnson continued, "I want to thank you, Mr. Bear—"

"Just 'Bear.'"

Johnson smiled. "Of course. I want to thank you, Bear, and you, too, Miss Rose, for all your help in the last two days. I know it was costly for you both."

"It was, at that." Bear agreed.

"And we will do what we can to make it up to you to the extent that it's humanly possible."

"There's no need for that," Bear said. "You and your people are certainly not to blame. As far as we're concerned, the Loward's Fury is responsible. They were coming after Rosie before we even met your people."

"All the same," Johnson said, "we'll do what we can to help you get started again."

Chubby arrived at the table with a tea tray loaded with all sorts of goodies. He put an oval dish of pot stickers in front of Rosie. "Here, Miss Rose, try these. If you like them, there are plenty more where these came from."

When Molly stuck her head up from under the table, Chubby placed a large plate full of odds and ends on the floor. Molly wagged her tail enthusiastically and fell to.

Rosie tasted a pot sticker cautiously, then froze while a smile of utter delight grew on her face. "I like them! A lot! What's in them?"

"Chicken and veggies, mostly." Chubby smiled at Rosie's obvious delight. "I'll go throw some more in the pan. Enjoy!"

As Johnson poured the hot tea for all of them, he continued, "For one thing, we'd really like to get you started making penicillin again. It *is* true that you can do that, right?"

"It's true. In fact, I've been supplying your medics for a while, through the black market. I guess Hank told you I lost my laboratory, but I suppose we can figure out something."

"Won't have to," Johnson said. "While you were recovering, I sent a salvage team to your old high school. They went through the wreckage and brought back everything of value that wasn't ruined." He smiled. "For what it's worth, we used those two military trucks you liberated from the Fury."

"That makes good hearing!" Bear said. "I lived there for more than thirty years, you know. There are some things I really didn't want to leave behind."

"Speaking of which—and I hope this meets with your approval—we gave your dog, Bruno, an honorable burial. We placed him by the other headstones."

Bear's voice grew thick. "Exactly right, and I'm grateful."

"Me too," Rosie said quietly, two large tears staining her cheeks.

In the ensuing silence, Chubby brought a second platter of pot stickers, placed it before Rosie, removed the empty plate, and returned to the kitchen without a word, a broad smile on his face.

Johnson said, "I have a rather large building over the river, across from our little hospital, that I've been reserving for something useful. Perhaps you'd like to have a look at it with me, see if it would be suitable for use as a laboratory. It has living quarters, too."

"Sounds good," Bear said. "I'll meet you there this afternoon if that's okay with you. I need to stop by the hospital and see Echo and JR."

"Works for me," Johnson said. "I'll see you there."

The Bear and The Rose

— Chapter 27 —

WOLF'S HEAD

WHEN ROSIE AND Bear arrived at the small, well-equipped hospital, they met JR limping down the walk. He sported a huge bandage on his right foot, necessitating the use of a crutch.

Rosie ran to JR and gave him a huge hug. "You're okay!" she said, smiling. "I'm so glad!"

"Kind-of okay," JR said in his quiet voice, "I'm missing all my toes on my right foot. The medics say I'm going to walk with a limp for the rest of my life. Still, all things considered, it could have been a lot worse."

"I'm in the same boat," Bear said. "This wound on my left leg gives me a limp. Medic says it's permanent, too, like yours. They gave me this walking stick. Said it's from before the War." Bear offered his walking stick for JR's examination. "Check out the handle. Nifty, don't you think?"

"A Golden Bear's head!" JR admired. "I'll say it's nifty! I wonder if I can get one like it when I get my bandages off."

"As it happens," Bear said, "they had another one like it, which I had them set aside for you."

"Another one?" JR asked. "With a bear's head?"

"Well, no," Bear said. "It has a silver wolf's head."

"A wolf's head," JR mused. "We'd be the Wolf and the Bear."

"You mean the Bear and the Wolf," Bear corrected, and they both laughed.

"Sure," JR agreed. "The Bear and the Wolf it is!"

"We're just going in to see Echo. Wanna come with?"

"I saw her this morning, early," JR said, "but sure, I'll come with you."

Bear told Molly to wait, then they went inside. The hospital occupied an entire industrial warehouse. At the nurse's station inside the door, a woman in a white uniform directed them to Echo's room.

Echo was mostly covered by a clean, white sheet. What little could be seen of her, her face and arms, was pale and gaunt. An IV dripped a clear solution into her arm.

Rat sat dozing in an armchair near the head of her bed. He roused himself when the gang came in. "Hi, guys. Hi, Bear, Rosie, JR. How're things?"

"Coming along," Bear said. "More to the point, how's Echo doing?"

"They say she's going to be fine. Just needs rest and hydration. I'm a little worried, though—she hasn't regained consciousness, and it's been a couple of days."

"What do the medics say?" Rosie asked.

"Mostly that she went through a really traumatic experience, and that she'll wake up when her mind and body are ready."

"Sounds right," Bear said. "She was unconscious the whole time she was with me, but there was some bad stuff going on around her. And that stuff can get in a person's head, even if they're unconscious."

"I think you must be right," Rat said, "because sometimes she says stuff in her sleep."

"Does she, now?" Bear asked. "What sort of stuff, if you don't mind me asking?"

"Hard to say," Rat replied. "She mentions the Iron Sceptre dude sometimes, but mostly she just moans and cries."

"She'll work it out," Bear said. "I've seen it before, in the War, with wounded soldiers. When her brain processes it all, she'll likely come around."

"I hope so," Rat said. "Because when she does, I'm going to marry her!"

"'Bout time," JR said with a grin. "You'd better name me your best man!"

"Who else?" Rat asked. "Then I'm going to join the Militia."

"Is the pay any good?" JR asked thoughtfully. "I thought the militia were mostly unpaid volunteers."

"They are," Rat said. "But the officers and non-coms get a small salary. Officers do a little better than the non-coms. Johnson came in yesterday and explained to me how the Militia works. He says, in view of my experience, I can start as a non-com."

"What's a non-com?" Rosie asked.

"A non-commissioned officer," Bear said. "Middle management. The officers make the decisions, then the non-coms carry them out."

"That's pretty much how Johnson explained it," Rat agreed. "So, we'll start our marriage with a house and a job."

"What house?" JR asked.

"Johnson says he'll find us a place in town. An apartment overlooking the river."

"So you'll start married life with a job and a house," Bear said. "Not bad."

"Beats scavenging," JR said.

"Yeah," Rat said. "That's for sure."

"We have to go," Bear said. "We're meeting Johnson and Hank across the street in a few minutes. There's a warehouse he wants me to look at."

"Okay," Rat said. "Thanks for looking in. I hope you'll come back soon?"

"We will, don't worry," Rosie said. "Give her a kiss from me when she wakes up. You and Echo are my family now."

"Mine, too," JR added. "And if you want me to spell you for a while, just let me know. I'd be happy to take a watch."

"Thanks," Rat said. "See you soon."

On the way out of the hospital, Bear stopped at the nurse's station and asked the duty nurse, "Hey, Darlene, do you still have that little item I asked you to keep for me?"

"Sure do, Bear," Darlene answered with a smile. From under the counter she produced a beautiful black walking stick with an exquisite silver wolf's head handle. "Here you go, JR. Bear said it's yours."

JR took the stick and spent a moment admiring the craftsmanship. "Thanks, Darlene. And thank you, Bear." He took a few tentative steps around the lobby. "This is going to make a tremendous difference in my quality of life!"

"It makes you look more dignified," Rosie said. "More mature, somehow. You two are quite the pair—the Bear and the Wolf!"

"I like that," JR said. "I guess I could be a wolf. But it's not like I was a real soldier."

"You sure could," Rosie said, which caused JR to blush. "And you are, too, a real soldier."

"It's true," Bear said. "Your wound might not have been received in actual combat, but it is nevertheless an honorable wound received from the enemy during wartime. Torture counts, too."

"Well…"

"'Well' nothing!" Rosie said. "In my book, you're a hero. They didn't make you talk, did they?"

"Well, no…"

"Then there you are!" Bear said. "The Rose has spoken, so walk with pride, man, walk with pride."

— Chapter 28 —

Bear's Place

Bear, Rosie, JR, and Molly left the hospital and walked across the boulevard to the industrial park where they were to meet Johnson to discuss Bear's new facilities.

Hank was waiting for them. "Hi, Bear, Miss Rose. Glad to see you've been discharged from the hospital, JR."

"They fixed me up as well as they could," JR said. "But I'm going to have a limp."

"I'm sure it'll improve in time," Hank said. Then to Bear, "Johnson's running late. Some problem with one of the families in town. He asked me to show you around until he could get here."

The facility turned out to be another large industrial warehouse/office combination, much like the hospital, and much larger than Bear was expecting.

"Are you excited about your new place?" Hank asked. "Johnson says that it's all yours to do with as you see fit, though he hopes you'll use at least part of it for manufacturing penicillin. We could sure use some."

"We'll see," Bear said. "Let's have a look first."

Hank unlocked the glass front door of the office portion of the building and ushered everyone inside. There wasn't much to see—it was just an office, with a few desks and chairs scattered about a worn, but clean, beige commercial carpet.

"There's a restroom in the corner over there," Hank said. "Everything works! Water, power, everything. There's solar on the roof."

Molly checked out every corner of the office, including the restroom, then came to announce her approval to Bear and Rosie, tail wagging.

"What do you think, Molly?" Bear asked. "Think we can make a place for ourselves here?"

Molly trotted over to the door leading to the warehouse portion and sniffed.

"She wants to see the warehouse before we decide," Bear said, and went through the door into the huge, high-ceilinged structure.

A stairway led to the mezzanine floor above the office area. A restroom occupied the corner under the stairway on the other side of the wall from the office restroom.

"No shower," Bear said.

"No kitchen, either," Rosie observed.

"Not down here," Hank said. "Don't worry about details. I have instructions to customize the interior to your specifications. Anyway, there are two full apartments above the office. Why not go on up and have a look?"

Each of the upstairs apartments was a complete living quarters, with a kitchen, a full bath, a living room, two bedrooms, and plenty of closet space.

"It's nice enough," Rosie said, "but there are no windows. I'm not sure I want to have my baby in a house without sunlight."

"How would you like to have a house of your own downtown?" Johnson said. "Sorry I'm late—had to take care of a minor dispute in town."

"Hello, Johnson," Bear said cordially. "Hank's been showing us around."

"What do you think of the place?" Johnson asked.

"Well, it's big enough for just about anything," Bear said. "All depends on what we plan on doing here."

"What *you* plan on doing here, Bear," Johnson said. "I'm just offering the space. I'm sure you noticed that there are plenty of places like it here in the industrial area. If you don't like this one, we can find you another one. Anyway, it's up to you how you decide to use it. I'm not the boss of anything, you know. It's not like I own any of this stuff."

"Who does own it, then?" JR asked.

"It's all left over from the War," Johnson said. "It belongs to whomever can make use of it, I suppose. What about it, Bear? Do you think you can find a use for the place?"

Bear smiled. "Oh, I think so. Especially if you can spare some of your guys to help me outfit the interior."

"Not a problem. I'm sure the Militia would be delighted to help you with anything you need."

"Excuse me, Mr. Johnson," Rosie said. "I'd like to hear more about that house in town you mentioned."

"It's just 'Johnson.' Like it's just 'Bear.' I had another name, a long time ago, but no one ever uses it anymore, not even me."

"Okay," Rosie said. She smiled. "'Johnson' it is, then. About that house…"

"There's an upstairs apartment above one of the buildings in town. It's not too far from Rat and Echo's apartment. It's small, but it's nice, and it has all the things: running water, a full bathroom, two bedrooms, kitchen. The best part, though, is that the front rooms have several large windows overlooking the river, all sunny and cheerful-like. It's a splendid view. I think you'd like it."

Bear frowned. "I hate to have to ask this, Johnson, but I need to know exactly what you are proposing. I'm not Rosie's father, as you know, but I am in what you might call loco parentis."

"Say no more," Johnson said. "My intentions are strictly honorable. The apartment would be Miss Rose's and hers alone. I have my own apartment over Chubby's place. And anyway, Rosie is still quite young."

"I'm not *that* young!" Rosie said with a twinkle in her eye. "And I don't mind older men. After all, Mr. The Bear, we were almost married, you and I—"

Bear gestured for Rosie to stop talking. "We're never, ever, *ever* going to mention that incident again, okay?"

Rosie giggled. "But you looked so cute without your—"

"NEVER MIND!" Bear roared. "Just forget it, okay?"

"Oh, I could never do that, Mr. The Bear. It's a sight I'll remember to my dying day! Besides, it explained so much."

"Like what?" Bear asked cautiously.

"Like why you look so big with your clothes *on*."

Everyone roared with laughter at that. Even Bear joined in, eventually. "All right, fine, whatever. Can we leave it alone now?"

"Of course, Mr. The Bear. For now, anyway." More giggling.

"Let me say again for the record," Johnson said, "this would be a strictly honorable arrangement, no strings attached. I understand Miss Rose is going to become a mother sometime soon, and in town, she'd have plenty of neighbor women to give her a hand."

"Please, Mr. The Bear? Say it's all right! I'd really love to have a place of my own!"

"Easy, there, Rosie Girl. We can have a look at it together, if you like. Anyway, remember what I told you about needing to learn to make up your own mind. As a mom, you're going to be functioning as an adult even if you are only fourteen. This is one of those adult decisions that you'll have to make for yourself."

Rosie threw her arms around Bear. "Thank you, Mr. The Bear! You are the best!"

"All right now, Rosie Girl. Let's get back to the business at hand, namely, whether or not I can use this facility, and if I even want to."

"Let me tempt you a bit further," Johnson said. "Hank, if you don't mind, could you tell the boys to come on in?"

"Sure thing!" Hank went out through the office.

After a brief interval, the pair of big, roll-up doors in the rear of the facility opened, and in came the two military trucks Bear had liberated from the Loward's Fury. The two trucks rolled to the middle of the giant warehouse and came to a stop. A pair of militiamen exited each vehicle and opened the rear cargo doors for Bear's inspection.

The first truck was full of all sorts of items brought over from Bear's former home: tools from the auto shop, the wood shop, and the metal shop; furniture and weapons from Bear's former quarters; massive amounts of food from the school's cafeteria; and laboratory equipment from the biology lab.

"We didn't bring the cold-storage items," Johnson said. "We'll fetch those when we get the coolers installed. The school's big freezers are still operating."

Bear, utterly speechless, went to look at the second truck's contents. Books! It was full of books. Thousands of them.

"Is... is this my entire library?" Bear asked quietly.

"The whole works," Johnson affirmed. "Except for a few dozen crates that wouldn't fit. We'll have to go back for those."

A soldier came forward and handed Rosie a small volume. "We found this on a bedside table in the ruins of the admin building. Thought it might be yours."

"Ah! There you are!" Rosie triumphantly held aloft her copy of The *Adventures of Robin Hood and His Merrie Men*. Her bookmark was right where she had left it. "Thank you, thank you very much! I was afraid I'd never find out what happened with that Robin fellow." She shook hands solemnly with the young militiaman, who blushed furiously, then ran to show the recovered tome to Bear. "I'll miss you if I'm living across the river."

"I'll miss you, too, Rosie Girl, but it doesn't have to be like that. Those apartments upstairs have two bedrooms. We can fix one of them up for you, and you can come stay over anytime you want, for as long as you want."

"Really?"

"Of course! Why not?"

"Well, for one thing, how am I going to get here? It's a long walk across the river, especially carrying a baby!"

"That won't be a problem," Johnson said. "Hank?"

Hank waved at a militiaman outside the back doors. A few seconds later, Bear's bright red 'shopping cart' zipped inside and rolled to a stop at Rosie's feet, all clean and shiny.

Rosie laughed. "I wondered what happened to your roller skate, Mr. The Bear!"

"We retrieved it from the high school where you left it," Hank said. "The boys and I cleaned it up. Looked like a family of pigs had recently moved out of it."

"Family of Bears, more likely," Rosie said, which made Bear scowl.

"If it's all right with you, Bear," Hank said, "we can just let Rosie use this thing. We'll fix you up with something more your size." He looked Bear up and down dubiously, making Rosie giggle. "Maybe a freight truck."

Bear sighed a long, sad, mock sigh. "I suppose," he said heavily. "We'll have to rig a charger for it here, though."

Rosie hugged Bear again. "Thank you, Mr. The Bear! I'll come see you all the time, I promise!"

"You'd better," Bear growled. "And another thing, while I'm thinking of it: that kid of yours had better call me Grandpa, if he knows what's good for him."

"Oh, he will, for sure!"

Bear scratched his head thoughtfully. "Say, Hank—where did my friend Brad end up?"

"Oh, she's over at the Militia HQ, just around the corner. We had quite a time talking Molly out of it. She seemed determined to wait for you right there at the boat landing. She wouldn't get out, but eventually she let us drive it back here. We had to get JR to come get her and take her to your hospital room. Anyway, the Bradley needed to be tidied up and refueled. As it happens, we had a bit of extra diesel. You want her over here?"

"Nah, not really. Brad's probably better off over at HQ. Here's an idea for you, though: maybe you should give some thought to training a couple of tank crews. I'm getting too old for that sort of thing, and I don't really picture Rosie, here, in the gunner's seat with a baby in her arms." He considered. "You know, Rat might make a good tank commander, in time."

Hank grinned. "I was hoping you'd say that. Naturally, Brad is strictly yours and will remain at your disposal whenever you wish."

Bear nodded. "Good, thanks, Hank. Makes sense to me. Probably won't want her very often, though. Looks like I'm going to be plenty busy getting this place set up."

"So you're going to take it?" Johnson asked.

"Looks like," Bear said. "I'm going to need some help, though."

"I could help," JR said. "I'm not going to be much of a soldier with this gimpy leg. I'd love to help get your lab running again."

"I'd like that," Bear said. "While you're at it, how about you fix up that second apartment for yourself? That'll make it convenient for you to get to work every day."

"Really?" JR said. "You mean it?"

"Sure," Bear said. "I'm going to need an assistant. There's a lot of work to do, establishing a new company, particularly a pharmaceutical company. "Wolf & Bear Laboratories, how does that sound? We'll make a good team. Also, there's no way I'm doing all this work by myself. I'm too old and too cranky for that. Say, Hank, you wouldn't happen to have some kind of architect on your staff, would you? How about sending him around to meet with JR and me? We can figure out what this place is going to need."

The Bear and The Rose

— Chapter 29 —

THE LOWARD'S OWN

A MONTH AFTER THE Battle of the Tabernacle, Johnson set aside a few blocks of vacant, pre-War houses for any of the Loward's Fury who might have survived.

Bear and Captain Skeeter counseled strongly against it, citing the young Fury soldier who had been corrupted by a desire for perverted sex and cannibalism and had proved unable to overcome his former way of life. Johnson shared their concerns but maintained that they had an obligation to show mercy to the defeated.

Bear, along with Captain Skeeter and Hank, reluctantly agreed to give it a try, but adamantly declared their intention to eliminate any survivor who showed signs of reverting to their previous behavior. Fortunately, the situation never arose, as no survivors ever came forward. Which suited Bear just fine.

It also left an entire neighborhood uninhabited. After a few more months had gone by, Johnson, at Rosie's request, sent a delegation of Militiamen, led by Hank, to Rosie's home neighborhood of Diablo, to offer assistance to any of the Loward's Own that might still exist, and invite them to take up residence in the vacant housing. All agreed that the Diablos, as they came to be called, were basically harmless, never having been part of the Loward's Fury or disciples of the Iron Sceptre, at least as far as anyone knew.

Hank returned with a handful of survivors, members of several families. Among them was Rosie's mother. "I'm sorry, Miss Rose," he explained later, "but your father refused to come. In fact, he wouldn't talk to us at all, after he found out who we were."

"Did you tell him about me?" Rosie asked.

"No, Miss Rose. I figured you could tell him yourself later if you wanted to. Didn't tell your ma, either. In fact, we didn't tell those poor folks anything much at all, only that there were houses, food, and medical care available to them at no cost if they wanted."

"I don't want to see my mother," Rosie said. "And, in a way, I'm glad my father didn't come. Without him, my mother might have some chance of getting better."

"Well," Hank said, "they've all been bathed, deloused, given new clothes, and fed. We burned their old clothing. I forgot to tell the cooks they were vegans, so they got chicken stew with biscuits for their first meal. No one objected, not a single word. And that stew didn't last long, either. When I left, the medics were making their rounds, checking everyone over. I'm sure your mother will be well cared for."

"Thank you for letting me know, Hank," Rosie said. "How about the children?"

"There were no children," Hank said. "We asked, but no one wanted to talk about it. It's possible they were taken by the Iron Sceptre at some point." Hank paused, scuffing at the wooden floor with the toe of his boot.

"What is it, Hank?" Rosie asked.

"It just—well… are you *sure* you don't want to see your mama?"

"I'm sure. Not right away, anyhow. Maybe after she has a chance to get back to herself again. There is one thing, though:

I'd like to make sure that the Diablos are assigned a teacher. They need to learn about the world, and the War, and Johnson, and what the future looks like. Otherwise, how can they have any part in it?"

"That's a good thought, Miss Rose. I'll bring it up next time I meet with Johnson, which will probably be tonight or else tomorrow morning. I'm sure we can find someone willing to spend time with those poor folks."

"Some of them are pretty good with their hands," Rosie said. "Maybe you can put them to work growing some food. Raising chickens, maybe. Or even a milk cow." She laughed. "Say, Hank—can you do me a favor? Make sure that teacher knows about the five basic food groups, okay?"

"Sure thing, Miss Rose. But I don't get it—why is that funny?"

"Why, don't you know, Hank? The first thing I learned after I met Mr. The Bear is that the cheeseburger is the perfect food!"

"Is that right?" Hank asked, scratching his head. "Well, I don't get the joke, but I'll pass it on to Johnson."

"Thanks, Hank. Say, while you're at it, that might be a good place for Billy, don't you think?"

"Good thought, Miss Rose. I'll mention that to Johnson, too. Might just be that Billy would appreciate a good home."

216

— Chapter 30 —

Larkin

A full six months after the Battle of the Tabernacle, Rosie's time was getting close. So close, in fact, that Rosie's girth prevented her from joining Bear, Hank, Captain Skeeter, and Johnson in their regular booth at Chubby's Chinese Kitchen.

Chubby, however, was well prepared for the situation, and provided a special plush, padded chair for Rosie's exclusive use, enabling her to sit across the table from Bear.

"What'll it be, Miss Rose?" Chubby asked. "The usual? I whipped up a special batch of pork pot stickers last night, just for you. I heard you might come in today."

At the sound of Chubby's voice, Molly's tail thumped against the wooden floorboards. "Don't worry, Molly," Chubby said. "I see you down there. I'll bring you something, too."

"That sounds wonderful, Chubby," Rosie said, rubbing her distended belly, "but I think I'll have to pass. I'm just not feeling so great today."

"You're not getting sick, are you?" Bear asked. "Tell me you're not getting sick."

"Of course I'm not getting sick," Rosie grumped, "unless you count being sick and tired of being an elephant!"

"Oh, now, Rosie Girl," Bear soothed, "you're not nearly as big as an elephant."

"More like a hippo," Johnson said.

"Or a rhinoceros, even," Hank suggested.

"Ha ha, very funny," Rosie said. "I really do feel huge today, though."

"Don't fret, Rosie," JR said as he came through the bat-wing doors. "It can't last much longer, right?" He dragged up another chair and sat next to her.

"I hope not," Rosie said, then doubled over. "Ooof! That's a bit of a cramp."

Captain Skeeter said, "Be careful what you wish for." There was a note of concern in his voice.

"I guess," Rosie said. She wiped the sweat from her forehead with a paper napkin. "Probably just another one of those practice contractions Mr. The Bear was telling me about." But then she frowned and doubled over again.

Molly leaped to her feet as a puddle formed under the table, which she sniffed carefully.

"Not so much with the 'practice' part, it seems," Bear said. "I do believe your water has broken. Congratulations! You're about to become a mother!"

"Yay!" Rosie said through clenched teeth. When the contraction had passed, she stood up. "I'd better head home."

"Probably so," Bear said. "But don't get in too much of a hurry. It'll likely be quite a while before the baby comes. 'Quality Work Takes Time,' remember. Walk slowly and carefully, take it easy. Especially on the stairs."

Rosie nodded. All of them, including Chubby, walked Rosie to the door and down the old wooden sidewalk, a few steps at a time, occasionally pausing for a contraction.

A young girl passing by stopped to watch Rosie's progress, and worked out what was going on. Her eyes grew wide, and Hank put a finger to his lips to warn her to keep quiet.

So, naturally, she began yelling at the top of her lungs, "Miss Rose is having her baby! Miss Rose is having her baby!" She ran off down the street, still squalling. The cry was taken up by the townsfolk, and by the time Rosie reached the foot of the stairs to her apartment, a small crowd had already gathered.

Hank and Captain Skeeter cleared a path, while Bear and JR helped Rosie up the stairs.

Rosie whispered to JR, "Send someone to get Rat and Echo, okay? Tell them to just come on up. You, too. Oh—and I guess you had better find Sally the Midwife if you can."

"Sure thing, Rosie," JR said. "No worries. Easy does it. I'll be back in a while."

They got Rosie upstairs and into a comfy robe. Bear made some tea and gave Rosie a mug with a little honey in it.

By and by, Sally the Midwife arrived. She checked Rosie's progress and announced that it was going to be a while yet, so everybody should just relax. Then she took Bear aside.

"What's up, Sally?" Bear asked.

"You saw me just now examine the girl, right?" she asked in a low voice.

"Sure. Everything okay?"

"Well, yes and no. Her labor is progressing nicely, but I couldn't help noticing that she's still a virgin."

Bear nodded slowly. "I expected that, based on what she told me of her parents' weird religion."

Sally raised her eyebrows but refrained from commenting.

"Tell you what," Bear said. "Let's you and me just keep that to ourselves, considering what happened last time there was a virgin birth."

Sally failed to get the reference. She merely shrugged and went about making her preparations.

Next, Rat and Echo came along, very excited. In just three months more, it would be Echo's turn to have her baby, so she and Rat had a special interest in Rosie's birth.

Bear and JR put themselves in charge of food and snacks, so there was always something available for everyone. Chubby kept sending huge platters of pot stickers and other Chinese finger foods until they had to send someone to tell him to stop. Rosie, of course, wasn't eating, but she was enjoying a bucket of chipped ice that Chubby had sent over from the restaurant's ice machine.

About the time the afternoon sun required closing the living-room blinds, Rosie's labor cranked up a couple of notches and the contractions began in earnest. The midwife ordered everyone out, but Rosie insisted that her friends remain for the occasion.

Rat and JR arranged some chairs in a circle around the edge of the living room. Rosie was comfortably ensconced on a mattress in the center of the floor. The midwife reminded everyone that, when the baby emerged, there was to be no shouting, cheering, yelling, or other loud noise, lest the baby be alarmed.

And so it was that on a quiet, sunny September afternoon, Rosie's firstborn son, Larkin, entered the world. Sally the Midwife looked little Larkin over, wrapped him in a blanket and held him up for all to admire, then passed him to Rosie to be nursed. Larkin seemed pleased to have finally arrived and got busy filling himself with his mother's milk.

While everyone was patting everyone else's back and offering mutual congratulations, the midwife was attending Rosie to ensure that all of the post-birth processes were proceeding correctly. And then, "Hang on, everyone! I think… yes… there it is… there's another one! Rosie's having *twins*!"

Sure enough, in due course, another infant's cry filled the room, and Sally the Midwife wrapped little Rork in a blanket and presented him to his mother. Rork joined his older brother at the milk bar.

When both infants had finished nursing and gone to sleep, Rosie, too, drifted off. Sally suggested that it would be a good time for all to take their leave and allow mother and babies some time to recover and start getting acquainted. Everyone whispered their goodbyes, gathered their belongings, and tiptoed out the door.

"You stay," Sally said to Bear. "I've got something to say to you."

"All right," Bear said, sitting himself back down. "What can I do for you?"

"It's the first baby, Larkin. Did you notice anything unusual about him?"

"Not really, no," Bear said. "Why?"

"I'm nearly certain that he's… he's…"

"What?" Bear said, becoming alarmed. "Is there something wrong with him?"

"Well… I think he's a… a little person."

"A little person? Of course he's a little person—he was just born!"

"No, not that. I mean, he's a dwarf."

"A dwarf."

"Yes. Normal body, short arms and legs."

"A dwarf," Bear said again. "Hunh. Does Rosie know?"

"She does now," Rosie said from her bed. "What exactly does this mean? Will he be stupid? I knew this one kid, back in Diablo…"

"No," Bear said, "not at all. He'll have a normal mind and body, but his arms and legs will be short. Apart from that, he'll have a relatively normal life."

"Relatively?" Rosie asked.

"He will have to learn to live in a world full of people who are taller than he is. But he'll have a lot of friends to help him do that. Meanwhile, he'll need plenty of love and care, the same as his brother."

Rosie smiled. "I think we can just about manage that. Don't you?"

"Of course I do," Bear said. "And I'll tell you something else: they'd *both* better call me Grandpa Bear, or I'll tan their little hides for them."

— Chapter 31 —

Epilogue

On a pleasant, sunny afternoon, nearly a year after the Battle of the Tabernacle, Bear and JR, with Captain Skeeter and Hank, commandeered one of the army transport trucks 'donated' to the Militia by the Loward's Fury. After filling it with all kinds of fresh fruits and vegetables, they parked it in front of Rosie's apartment. Bear and JR waited with the dogs while Captain Skeeter and Hank helped Rosie, her mother, and Billy bring the twins downstairs. They had to make a second trip for more goodies that Rosie and her mother had prepared. Next, they made another stop to pick up Rat and Echo at their little house, along with yet another load of picnic foods.

Molly and her six pups rode in the back with Rat, JR, and Billy. Bear had given Molly strict instructions to stay out of the picnic baskets, no matter how tantalizing the smell. Molly, as always, was the very model of intelligent canine obedience, but she kept busy keeping her offspring away from the goodies, with an occasional nip of an ear or a warning growl. The pups were good sports about it—they'd been on picnics before and knew the drill. After all, they were nearly grown now, almost a year old.

Bear drove them across the ancient Tower Bridge, which had been old even before the War. The section between the two towers, Bear explained, was something called a drawbridge. It was supposed to rise to allow tall boats to pass under, but Bear doubted that the mechanism was still in working order. That was something the Militia's engineers might look into one day.

North along the river, they found a large, green, grassy park, another pre-War relic, complete with recently rebuilt picnic tables, some fire pits, and a working restroom, courtesy of the Militia's engineers.

Everyone pitched in, of course, and before long, the celebratory feast was deployed on several of the picnic tables that Captain Skeeter and Hank had pushed together. When everyone was seated, Bear raised his glass. "To family, and to a bright and hopeful future for our children, born and as yet unborn." With that, everyone began serving everyone else all the goodies.

"Too bad your father couldn't be here," Bear said to Rosie, "but I'm glad to see your mother made it. She's looking good these days. Are you two getting along all right?"

"Mostly all right, Mr. The Bear," Rosie said through a mouthful of potato salad. "She has good days and bad days. This is one of her good days. On her bad days, she sometimes forgets who she is, or where she is. Sometimes she gets upset because she can't find my father."

"He still refuses to come in?" Rat asked.

"He's very stubborn," Hank said. "The last time I was out there he chased me away with a shovel."

Rosie giggled. "Yep, that's my dear old dad. How did he look?"

"Not too well," Hank said. "He's starving, a walking skeleton."

"That's a shame," Bear said, "when he could be enjoying all this bounty."

"And his grandsons," Rosie's mother said, then her face clouded over. "Except, they're not really his, are they?"

"We've been over this, Mother," Rosie said. "I'm their mother, so he's their grandfather. We just don't know who the *father* is. Or fathers, maybe. There's no way to know and no way to find out. We'll probably never know."

"Before the War," Bear said, "there was a thing called genetic testing. By reading the genetic code in your cells, you could tell if you were related to someone or not. But I haven't heard of anyone still doing that."

"Me neither," Captain Skeeter said. "Wouldn't help Rosie, anyway. Don't you have to have some genetic material from the possible fathers?"

"That's right," Bear said. "From what I understand of the Loward's Own's rituals…"

"Let's change the subject, Mr. The Bear, if you don't mind. I'd rather look ahead than behind, especially today."

"Of course, Rosie Girl. You're absolutely right. Very insensitive of me. How is little Larkin keeping up with his brother?"

"Larkin's fine," Rosie said. "So far, he seems completely unaware that he's different."

"By the time he's old enough to realize, he'll already have the skills he needs to cope, I'm sure," Captain Skeeter said. "Plus—" he gestured around the table "—he'll have plenty of family to guide him."

"In another little while," Echo said, "He'll have another small friend." She patted her belly proudly. "Sally the Midwife says that I'm coming along just fine, perfectly normal."

"We're pretty excited," Rat said. "Three more months to go! Can't wait to find out if it's a boy or a girl! I hope whichever it is, it'll get along with the dog."

"Thank you again for the puppy, Bear," Echo said. "Zenia is a very good girl. We love her!"

Upon hearing her name, Zenia put her head in Echo's lap, then asked for a treat. Echo found her a little bit of bacon.

After a while, when they had eaten their fill, Captain Skeeter, Bear, and Rosie found themselves together, sitting in the shade of a majestic elm tree, watching the babies play. Rat and Echo, hand in hand, walked along the riverbank, talking and laughing.

"I think we did the right thing," Bear said.

"What's that?" Captain Skeeter asked.

"Not telling Echo what happened to her at the tabernacle."

"I agree," Rosie said. "It only would have upset her, and there wasn't any need for her to know."

"You mean… ?" Captain Skeeter asked.

"I found out, in casual conversation, that she was having her periods normally when she and Rat got married," Rosie said. "So I didn't see any point in bringing up the past."

Bear nodded thoughtfully. "She would have carried the 'burden of knowledge' her entire life."

"Might even have messed up her marriage," Captain Skeeter said, "though I have a lot of confidence in young Rat. He's a good kid, turning into a fine soldier. I'm proud of him. Still, the knowledge of the rape would have saddened him for the rest of his life, too."

"They sure look happy together now," Bear said. "And I'm glad about that."

A while later, Rosie's mother came and sat with them for a while. Billy, of course, came with her, his 'lead rope' tied about his waist, as usual. As they talked, Billy plucked little bits of grass and sticks and put them in his mouth.

While Echo spoke with Rosie's mother, Captain Skeeter quietly asked Rosie, "What's with the rope? Is she afraid he'll get lost? What happens when he gets loose?"

"It's not like that," Rosie said. "Billy wants it that way. In fact, he refuses to leave the house without his tether. I think he feels safer with it on."

"How about that," Bear said. "And your mom's okay with that?"

"Sure. For her, it's like having another kid. Kinda makes up for me running away from them, I guess."

"Except," Captain Skeeter added, "Billy is unlikely to ever grow up enough to object."

"I feel bad about that," Bear said. "Well, a little, anyway. I'm afraid I caused it by hanging him upside-down in the Bradley."

"I don't think so, Mr. The Bear," Rosie said. "I think he must have been simple-minded to start with. I think you saved his life."

"Being in the restroom saved his life," Bear said.

"Which is a lesson to us all," Captain Skeeter said, which made everyone laugh. "Actually, Miss Rose, you're the one who saved him. I was ready to put him out of his misery. It was only your intervention… Strange to think that Billy is the last remnant of the Loward's Fury. I, for one, won't miss them one bit."

"Well," Rosie said, "I hope it turns out for the best. They seem happy, Billy and my mother, so maybe it'll be all right after all." She looked around, then stiffened. "Where *is* my mother, anyway? Did she take my babies?"

"She's fine," Bear said. "She's right over there, by the water."

Rosie's mother had taken the two babies down by the riverside, where she was rocking sleeping Rork in her lap while Larkin was throwing little bits of grass and sticks toward the river.

Rosie walked over to join her mother who was tenderly stroking Rork's hair and singing a lullaby as he slept. Rosie's blood froze when she drew close enough to make out the words:

> Someday you will be the king,
> And the old Gods you will bring.
> The Iron Sceptre will return,
> Your fires will make the children burn.

About the Author

Connor MacKenzie was born in the United States in 1956. After graduating from high school, Connor declined a medical scholarship to Stanford University. Instead, Connor traveled the world working at many jobs, including all of the construction trades, window washer, hot-air balloon pilot, house painter, time-share salesman in Mexico, school bus driver, street musician, English teacher in the Dominican Republic, ranch hand, e-zine publisher, bio-diesel manufacturer, sailboat captain, carpet cleaner, pig photographer, and computer programmer. He now resides on California's North Coast, where the redwoods meet the sea.

Also by Connor MacKenzie:

The Proud Old Name, Special Enhanced Edition
(editor and historian)